Graduate Learning Clinic
Education Department
Nazareth College of Rochester
4245 East Avenue
Rochester, NY 14618-3790

wolf

ON THE

fold

Also by Judith Clarke

wolf

ON THE

folD

Judith Clarke

FRONT STREET

Asheville, North Carolina

First published by Silverfish, an imprint of Duffy & Snellgrove, in 2000
Published by Allen & Unwin in 2001
Copyright © 2000 by Judith Clarke
Printed in the U.S.
Designed by Helen Robinson
First U.S. edition 2002

Library of Congress Cataloging-in-Publication Data
Clarke, Judith
Wolf on the fold / Judith Clarke
p. cm.
Summary: A series of stories that follows members of an
Australian family through several generations.
ISBN 1-886910-79-0 (alk. paper)
[1. Family life-Australia-Fiction. 2. Australia-Fiction.] I. Title.
PZ7.C55365 Wo 2002
[Fic]-dc21 2001059750

For Frances Sutherland

family tree

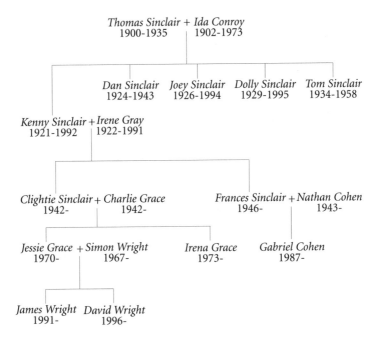

Thomas Sinclair + Ida Conroy
1900-1935   1902-1973

Dan Sinclair   Joey Sinclair   Dolly Sinclair   Tom Sinclair
1924-1943   1926-1994   1929-1995   1934-1958

Kenny Sinclair + Irene Gray
1921-1992   1922-1991

Clightie Sinclair + Charlie Grace
1942-   1942-

Frances Sinclair + Nathan Cohen
1946-   1943-

Jessie Grace + Simon Wright
1970-   1967-

Irena Grace
1973-

Gabriel Cohen
1987-

James Wright   David Wright
1991-   1996-

contents

wolf on the *fold*

1935

It was the middle of winter and the middle of the Great Depression on the morning Kenny Sinclair set out to find a job.

He was just fourteen. Three weeks ago his dad had died, fallen down in the back garden where he was digging a trench for the potatoes. "Heart," the doctor had said. "Like a tree," Kenny had heard his mum telling Uncle Albert at the funeral. "He went down like a tree."

There were four children in the family besides Kenny: Dan and Joey, who were eleven and nine, Dolly, who'd turned five last October, and the baby, Tom. The Sinclairs had always been poor and scraped along as best they could; now they were poorer still. The need to get money—for food, and for rent on the old house on

Cross Street—was like an iron bar laid flat across their necks, squashing their faces down into the ground. Even the baby—Mum said he was too young to understand, but he did know something, you could see. He stayed awake in the crib beside the stove, watching them silently, his round, dark eyes grown larger, sliding from face to face.

The baby would be all right, though. If worse came to worst, little Tom would get to stay with Mum. The weight fell most heavily on Kenny, who had to leave school and find work. He didn't mind leaving; he hated school anyway: the shouting, the dull drone of recitation, the whizzy whack of the cane. He hated especially the smell of the cold back stairs, like chalk and a slaughteryard—first thing on a Monday morning, it made you want to be sick.

He'd rather be out working. All the boys said this, chumming together behind the shelter shed at recess, kicking their heels, chafing at the useless hours spent learning stuff that wouldn't be a speck of use out there beyond the school. Only it was different now for Kenny because he had to; it wasn't talk anymore but that cold weight of iron pressing down upon his neck.

He had to find work or the family would get split up; Nan could only take Mum and Tom, and Uncle Albert didn't want any of them. Dolly, it seemed, could go to

Aunty Trish, Dad's sister down in Melbourne. Mum seemed unhappy with this idea; Melbourne was so far away and Mum had only met Aunty Trish once, long ago when she'd come up for Granddad's funeral. She hadn't come to Dad's. They all felt in their bones that if Dolly went to live with Aunty Trish they might never see her again. Never to see Dolly again—how could such a thing ever happen? But they knew it could, because they knew anything might happen now.

And Aunty Trish and Uncle George were different from them. They were rich. They lived in a big house beside the river, a house they owned instead of renting; they had a car, and their kids went to private schools. "She'd be treated like a little servant," Mum whispered to Kenny when his brothers and sister were out of earshot. "Though I suppose it's better than a Home."

Anything was better than a Home. A Home was where Dan and Joey would have to go, and Kenny too, if he couldn't find work. Dan and Joey said they wouldn't go—never never never! They had this idea of running away to sea, getting taken on as cabin boys in ships that sailed around the world. Because Kenny was older, he knew this idea was no more than a dream, the stuff of boys' adventure books. It was rubbish, rubbish the pair of them talked up when they got scared in the middle of the night.

You only had to think about it for a second—what ship would take on Dan and Joey, young and runty as they were? Joey wore thick hospital glasses, one lens pasted with brown paper to correct his faulty sight. Dan looked eight instead of eleven, and he was the kind of loud-mouthed, squawky kid that older boys bashed up on sight. Even if a miracle happened and some kind captain took them on, the sailors would chuck Dan overboard the minute the ship left port.

Dan and Joey would never be able to find their way to the sea: it was miles away and if they ran off they'd only get lost. Like Dolly if she went to Melbourne, they might never be seen again.

Kenny's mum woke him early, that morning he set out to look for work. When he came into the kitchen, his head still thick with sleep, she had the stove alight already and a big pot of porridge simmering on the top. The room seemed lovely to him, warm as a blessing; and it was ages since he'd been alone with Mum like this, sitting with her over breakfast without the other kids around.

She'd given him the creamy top of the milk on his porridge and a sprinkle of rich brown sugar, and his bowl was full to the brim. Hers wasn't; her bowl was only half full, or less. She'd got like this since their dad had died, giving everything to him and the other kids, making the food go round among the lot of them, leaving herself out. Dad wouldn't have liked her doing this, Kenny knew. He'd have loved her for it, with the same harsh, painful love Kenny felt right now, a love that held a spark of anger deep inside—but he wouldn't have liked it, the way it made you feel guilty and wrong inside.

When she got up to fill the kettle and her back was turned, Kenny, moving quickly, spooned extra porridge from his bowl to hers. She noticed it the moment she sat down; Kenny felt the flick of her eyes toward his face. "Don't!" he urged her silently. "Don't say anything. And don't give it back, please!" He wanted her to have it; he felt it was the only thing he had to give until he found work, and that might not be for a long, long time. It mightn't be in time.

She said nothing. She picked up her spoon and began to eat, and then Kenny started eating too.

The small, sticky grains of the porridge got under his teeth; the teeth rocked slightly, then slid back into place again.

They were new teeth. Not new like little Dolly's, growing strongly from her pink young gums—Kenny's teeth were new in a different, awful way. A few weeks back, just before his dad died, Kenny had copped a cricket ball right in the mouth; it had knocked out four front teeth. The dentist down on Station Road had taken out the lot of them; it was cheaper that way, he'd said, since Kenny's other teeth were full of holes. "You'd lose them by the time you were twenty anyway," he'd added. "They'd only be a trouble to you; they're better out than in."

Kenny hated the new teeth; he hated the way they shifted when he ate, and sometimes even when he talked. His speech was different now, muffled and unclear; it had been awful at school with the kids laughing and Mr. Blewitt thinking he was mumbling on purpose and shouting at him to speak up. He hated the look of his face in the mirror when he took them out: shriveled as a gnome's. And today, this very morning, hardly more than an hour away, he would have to pre-sent himself to strangers behind the gates of factories; he would have to speak up clearly, tell them he wanted a job.

A wave of panicky terror engulfed Kenny there at the kitchen table; his hand trembled as he lifted the next spoonful of porridge to his mouth.

"Kenny?" His mother had noticed the trembling hand. "Are you all right?"

"It's just—hot," he spluttered, blowing on the porridge, and she trickled in a little more milk from the jug. "Thanks," he murmured, and lowered his head down over the bowl.

The terrifying thing was how getting work was so important and at the same time completely hopeless.

Why should anyone give a kid like him a job, fresh from school, with no experience, when there were thousands out looking for work—grown men, fathers of families, laid off, unemployed? You saw them everywhere: outside the Royal on Station Road, selling clothes pegs, shoelaces, and razor blades from door to door. You heard them going by in the night, up Cross Street, heading for the highway and the bush, heard their footsteps and the eerie jingle of the pan and billy hanging from their blueys.

Grown men, they were. And he was only a kid of fourteen. He didn't even look fourteen, he was almost as scrawny as Dan. The whole thing swept over him in a rush: his dad dead and lying out in Rookwood, Dan and Joey in a Home, Dolly lost from them far away at Aunty Trish's, their house with other people in it—all because he couldn't get a job to pay the rent. In a few months, maybe even less, some other kid might be sitting at this very table eating his breakfast, thinking, when he looked around the room: my kitchen, my house, my home. Kenny wanted to drop his spoon and slam his hand down, *bang*, at the crazy injustice of it all; he wanted to scrape his chair back and run round the table to Mum, bury his head in her lap and start blubbing like he used to do when he was little and he hurt himself or things went wrong. He wanted to bawl out loud about how he'd never find work, not if he went looking for a whole long year, how he was too small, too young, and his teeth made him sound slow and stupid when he talked. But he knew he couldn't do that now; it wouldn't be fair to Mum. He couldn't ever do it again. Like Nan had said at the funeral, "You're the man of the family now."

They drank their tea in silence. It was beginning to get light. Through the window, Kenny could see the outline of the shed and the gum tree near the fence, and the pale moony blur of a sheet left hanging on the line. The night after Dad died, he and Dan had crept out into the yard and unpegged Dad's clothes from the line; they hadn't wanted Mum to look through the kitchen window and see them hanging there. They'd put them in an old cardboard box and hidden the box in the back of the laundry, covered with old rags. "Till she's feeling a bit better," Kenny had said, and Dan's face had crumpled up in misery. "When?" he'd asked, clutching at his brother's arm. "When?" Kenny hadn't known the answer to that; he didn't know it now.

He got up from the table and took his jacket from the nail behind the kitchen door. As he shrugged it on, his mother handed him a flat package wrapped in butcher paper. "Sandwiches," she said. "You'll need something to keep you going."

He nodded, tucking the parcel carefully inside the

pocket of his jacket, where it fitted exactly, like a birthday card inside its envelope. "Thanks," he said, and then there was nothing left except to go through the door and down the verandah steps to where the bike was propped ready against the laundry wall. It was his dad's bike, the one he'd used to ride to work, big and black and serviceable. Kenny had cleaned it up the night before, oiled the chain, pumped up the tires, and checked the small saddlebag for rubber patches in case he got a flat. It was a long way to the factories on the edge of town.

"Wait," called a voice from behind him, and he turned and saw his mum had followed him into the yard. She began to button up his jacket for him, right to the neck, like she used to do when he was little, barely older than Tom was now, and couldn't manage buttons for himself. It was so surprising, this small thing from long ago, that Kenny sucked in his breath and held it until she was done. "There," she said, fastening the very last button, giving his shoulder a pat, then standing back to look at him.

The color flushed up in his face. "I'll be off then," he muttered, leaning forward, aiming an awkward peck at her cheek, which missed and caught the tip of her cold nose.

"Good luck," she whispered. He wished she'd go back inside the house now and leave him to get on with it. But no, she had to follow him up the path to the front gate, and the moment he placed his foot on the pedal she laid her hand on his arm. "Be careful going through the flatlands," she said.

The flatlands was the long stretch of marshy country between their place and the suburbs where the factories began. It was a wasteland: miles of flat, soggy country riddled with tiny trickling creeks, crisscrossed by narrow tracks that went nowhere, wandering through thickets of blackberry and lantana, ending in bogs and brambles or great banks of quivering, rustling reeds. It was a lonely place where no one lived and where strange little winds blew, even on the stillest days.

"Careful?" he echoed.

"Be sure you keep to the road, Kenny. Don't go off it. And don't stop for anyone."

"There won't be anyone around this early," said Kenny, and then his mum replied that some people kept odd hours.

It was the word "odd" that made him realize she was talking about the man who'd taken those boys away. Two boys: one last week, and the other a month back now. They were dead, though he didn't know the details because Mum had hidden the paper. Leo Hicks, a boy from his school, said they'd been hacked up. "Slit 'em down the belly, gutted 'em like fish" was how Leo had put it, but you couldn't be sure he was right; Leo Hicks made things up. And even if Leo had been telling the truth—on this particular morning, with the search for work ahead of Kenny, the story seemed insubstantial as a fairytale. But his mother was looking straight into his eyes, wanting promises.

"I'll be careful," he said to her, and she nodded gravely, accepting his word. With a last light touch on his arm she stepped back to let him go. At the bottom of Cross Street, slowing to turn the corner, he looked back up the hill and saw she was still there, standing on the pavement beneath the streetlight, gazing after him, one arm upraised as if she were holding something up to the sky. He gave her one last wave and pedaled round the corner onto Station Road.

Long after his mother had died, whenever Kenny thought of her it was this image that came back: not the young woman she'd been when he was little, or the old lady his daughters had called Nan, but Mum standing outside the old house on Cross Street on that morning he went out to look for work, standing very still and straight, her arm upraised as if she were saluting him. The picture seemed very near, as close as yesterday, and when he woke from the memory, the place where he was felt wrong to Kenny. He might be mowing the lawn, and then his own backyard would look strange for a moment because he'd expected to see Cross Street early on a winter's morning. Or he might be inside the house, having a cuppa, and then his own kitchen would be a surprise because it should have been the kitchen in the old house—then Kenny would feel a strange little tremor of shock, as if some trick had been played on him.

That winter was the coldest for years out round their way; most mornings there was frost, a thin crust of ice on the grass. Cold made the hooves of the milkman's horse ring like bells, and the milk froze in the billycan. By the time Kenny reached the long, straight road through the flatlands he was frozen, and despair had settled in his heart like icy sludge. He knew he wouldn't get a job; they'd take one look at him and let him go. He would have to stand in line with men at the factory gates, he would have to talk to strangers in the offices and yards—and he was shy with adults, awkward with them.

He'd always been like that: tongue-tied, his nan called him. It amazed him to see the way young Joey could carry on conversations with grownups—so easily, as if it were the most natural thing in the world. Passing old Mrs. Gribbon's house, where she sat rocking on her porch, waiting for a word with passers-by, Joey would yell out, "G'day, Mrs. Gribbon! Lovely morning, eh?" When Kenny was Joey's age he'd been so scared of Mrs. Gribbon he'd take the long way home so he wouldn't have to pass her house. "You're like a stuttering person," Joey had told him once. "Except you haven't got a stutter."

His stupid teeth made it worse; Leo Hicks said he sounded mental, "like you've escaped from the loony bin." At his father's funeral, when they were putting Dad in the ground, with Mum standing there so white and still, and Dolly flinging herself down on the ground to scream, tugging out fistfuls of grass and scattering it all over her dress and hair—even then he'd kept on thinking about his teeth, hoping no one would come and talk to him so he'd have to open his mouth and answer in that stupid-sounding voice. He'd stood apart from them, half hidden behind a big gray tomb—and he shouldn't have done that; he should have stood beside Mum and helped her out with Dolly, instead of thinking about himself. Selfish, that had been. As if your teeth mattered when your dad had died...

And now, half frozen, pedaling along this lonely road, with the factories at the end of it, and all of them waiting at home, he was thinking about his teeth: how stupid they made him sound, and how awful it had been the first day he'd got them. They'd hurt so much he'd taken them out the minute he got home, he'd lain down on his bed with a towel over his mouth and the teeth beside him on the packing-case table. Then Joey and Dan had come bursting into the room; Dan had snatched the teeth from the table and clacked them together in a snapping bite. "Look! A crocodile!" he'd shouted. Then he'd put the top ones in his mouth, over his own teeth, and pranced and capered round the room, with Joey leaping beside him, snatching, screeching, "Give us! Give us a go!"

Kenny had thrown the towel off and leapt up shouting. His voice had been loud all right, but it mushed his words to simple noise; he'd sounded like an animal, and looked like one too, with the blood all round his mouth. Joey and Dan had backed away in fright.

That had been it, for Kenny. He'd made a vow: from that moment on, even if they hurt and hurt, he'd never take those teeth out where anyone could see. He'd wear them all the time, he'd sleep in them, like you weren't supposed to do—no one would ever catch him out again.

Kenny kept that promise all his life. He took his teeth out only to clean them, locking the bathroom door. His daughters Frances and Clightie never realized their father's teeth weren't real until he was an old man dying in a hospital bed and the nurses took his teeth away.

Then their father refused to see anyone except for them.

"No one's going to notice, Dad," pleaded Clightie, and Frances added, "No one's going to care that you haven't got your teeth."

"I care," said Kenny, and he wouldn't even see his brother Joey. Clightie rang Uncle Joey from the phone outside the ward. "It's his teeth, Uncle Joey," she sobbed. "They took them away and now he won't see anyone, not even you."

There was a long silence on the end of the line before Uncle Joey said slowly, "He never would let us look."

"Look?" repeated Clightie.

"At his teeth, when he got them, when we were kids. The two of us, your Uncle Dan and I—we used to tease him about them. We didn't know, you see. We didn't know how he felt. We were only kids and—"

Now there came another silence, longer than the first. "Uncle Joey?" cried Clightie. "Uncle Joey, are you there?" Uncle Joey had gone.

When their father was sleeping, Frances and Clightie sat on chairs outside his room and whispered together. Was their dad being silly, or was he being brave? Was it dignity he showed, or stubborn foolishness?

"I don't know," said Clightie, and she started crying again. "I just don't know."

Frances jumped up and caught at the sleeve of a passing nurse. "Why can't you give my dad his teeth back?" she demanded angrily. *"He's dying anyway, so what does it matter if he chokes on them?"*

The nurse was shocked. She pressed her lips together tightly, and hurried on without a word.

But that was a whole lifetime away on the morning Kenny rode through the flatlands on his father's old black bike. The lush grass by the roadside was a brilliant flashy green; lantana and blackberries ran wild. He passed no one on the road and the cold seemed to bring a great stillness to the world; he wouldn't have believed he was moving except for the whistling of the frozen air against his ears. He'd never known that cold could actually hurt like this: a painful block of ice inside his chest which burned each time he took a breath. His ears ached and water streamed stinging from his eyes. His nose hurt dreadfully at first. Now it had gone numb and he couldn't check that it was there because his hands seemed welded to the handlebars.

He had to keep going; there was nothing else he could do. He had to keep riding on, he had to reach the factories, he had to try and try; back at home, they were depending on him. A little way ahead he could see the culvert that meant he'd come halfway; he'd just passed it when he saw the fire, a small red glow not far in from the road. You saw those fires in the flatlands sometimes, left by the men passing through on their way off to the bush. Kenny's legs slowed above the pedals, the idea of a fire, of holding his frozen hands out to the warmth, thawing the numbness of his face, his nose...

It would only take five minutes, and he'd made good time, he knew; five minutes spent beside the fire would make no difference. If he thawed out a little he could pedal faster, the cold must be slowing him down. Kenny stopped, resting one foot on the road, gazing hungrily toward the fire.

"Don't stop," his mum had said. No, wait, it hadn't been "Don't stop"—what she'd said was "Don't stop for anyone." And there wasn't anyone, the road was deserted and he could tell by the silence at the back of everything —behind the bird calls and the rustling of the reeds— that there was no one in there beside that fire. The traveler who'd made it would have gone long ago; they always moved on at first light. He'd have left the fire burning because in winter it could do no harm.

Kenny turned his bike in from the road, laid it down behind a thicket of blackberry, and hurried up the narrow track. The tall grass brushed and sighed against his legs; a prickly tendril snatched at the stuff of his trousers.

"Be sure you keep to the road," his mum had said. "Don't go off it." Yes, she'd said that all right. He stopped. The fire was so close now. He could almost feel its lovely warmth pulsing through the air, like the kitchen this morning when he'd stepped inside.

He knew this place, this first track past the culvert. He and Leo Hicks had come here in the summer; they'd built a cubby in the very clearing where the fire burned. You could see the road from that clearing, that's how close it was. What Mum had meant, really, what she must have meant, was "Don't try and take a shortcut through the flatlands."

The paths he and Leo had followed last summer hadn't gone anywhere, they'd ended in the reeds. But people said there were tracks that led all the way to the suburbs on the other side—and that's what his mum had meant, of course: she'd been worried he'd get lost taking one of those, end up in reeds and brambles, have to double back and waste his time. Well, he wasn't doing that; he'd only take five minutes and then he'd be back on the road. Kenny walked quickly down into the clearing.

He was so intent on reaching the warmth that he didn't notice the man until he spoke. As Kenny stretched his hands out to the flames a voice came from the other side of the fire. "G'day," it said.

Kenny's head shot up; he peered through the drifting smoke and saw a figure hunched behind it, watching. "G-G'day," he stammered, and at once his mother's words came back to him—that when she'd said, "Some people keep odd hours," he'd known at once she meant the man who'd taken those kids away.

This couldn't be him, though, decided Kenny. The man she'd been afraid of wouldn't be here, so close to the road, lighting a fire, drawing attention to himself—not when the cops were hunting him. This was just an old tramp, too weary and slack to get up early and move on along the road. Kenny took a small step sideways, to see the stranger better. He wasn't old—no older than Kenny's dad had been, anyway. He wore an old brown coat, mud-stained trousers, and shoes tied up with string. He was the sort of man you saw in the street every day, his face was the kind you'd never notice; he didn't look cruel or bad.

"Cold out, eh?" the stranger said to Kenny.

The boy nodded.

"Fancy a cuppa?" The man gestured toward a blackened billy on the ground beside him.

"Nah," said Kenny. "I've gotta go in a minute. I only came to, to—"

"Get warm," the stranger finished, moving forward to stir the fire. "Be my guest," he murmured, and sparks like rubies flew into the air. "Out early this morning, aren't you?"

"I'm looking for work," mumbled Kenny.

"Oh dearie me."

The words sent a thrill of fright down Kenny's spine. They weren't strange in themselves, they were ordinary and familiar; he'd heard his nan say them often, when Tom grizzled, when Dolly fell down the steps and cut her knee. But they were wrong here, wrong from the stranger; they didn't fit what Kenny had said to him. They made no sense.

"Oh dearie me," the man said again. He grinned at Kenny, and the grin made his face wolfish.

The boy edged sideways, away. "Gotta go," he said thickly, trying to keep the panic from his voice. "I've gotta go now—"

He took a step and wasn't quick enough; the man's hand shot out and seized him by the ankle, fast. The stranger was strong—power hummed from his fingers like fierce electricity. He said nothing, he just held on, and his eyes traveled from Kenny's ankle up along his body to his face.

"Slit 'em down the belly, gutted 'em like fish," Leo Hicks had said.

This couldn't be that man. It couldn't be.

Kenny raised his head and met the stranger's eyes, full on. He was hoping for a joke of some kind: a smile on the shabby man's face, the fingers loosening to let him go. "Tricked you, eh?"

It didn't happen. There was no smile, no joking words; the stranger's blank face might have had nothing to do with the hand that held Kenny so fast. Except— there was something funny going on in his eyes. Gazing into them was the strangest experience: it was like looking down onto a battlefield where two great armies clashed, where swords rang and men and horses screamed and banners flew out in the wind. Lines of a poem he'd learned at school flashed into Kenny's mind: "The Assyrian came down like the wolf on the fold; / And his cohorts were gleaming in purple and gold…"

He'd never thought he'd remember those lines ever again once he was free of school. He'd hated poetry, hated how Mr. Blewitt made them learn it off by heart and whacked them when they got it wrong. And this poem was the one Kenny had hated most; Mr. Blewitt had almost pulled his ear off for saying *foal* instead of *fold*. "Foal's a baby horse, boy!" he'd roared. Kenny still didn't know what *fold* was.

The fingers round his ankle had tightened savagely. It didn't seem possible they were part of any human thing. Images blazed up in Kenny's head: his mum with her hand upraised, saluting him, Dan and Joey whispering together, making their plans to run away to sea, Dolly's little face, Tom's big round eyes. His fear of not being able to find work, his shyness, his stupid teeth—he saw now that these were mere specks of dust in the kingdom of his life. He needed that life; he had promises to keep. And the promise to find work seemed easy now; it was nothing to the greater one: how there had to be a Kenny who'd come home tonight, who'd walk in alive through their own kitchen door. He had to keep that promise first.

The battle raged on in the stranger's eyes. Kenny knew it would be no good to struggle, to pull away, cry out—the second he did that he'd be finished, slit down the belly, gutted like a fish—this was plain as day. With some deep, sure instinct he saw that his only chance lay in keeping still and quiet—a possum playing dead, a sky with no clouds in it—until the battle finished, the swords fell, the shouting died, and the banners drooped across the field.

And it was good that more lines of that poem came to Kenny then. Repeating those lines in his head helped him to keep still, to draw so far inside himself he mightn't have been there, might never have come there in the first place, ridden by without stopping, his tires humming on the road.

"The Assyrian came down like the wolf on the fold," chanted Kenny silently. "And his cohorts were gleaming in purple and gold; / And the sheen of their spears was like stars on the sea, / Where the blue wave rolls nightly on deep Galilee."

Yes, it was good the way those lines came rolling in to him.

Years on, when he was a father and a family man, it always made Kenny smile to think how that poem he'd hated had kept him going, kept him still and quiet in that iron grip, spared him, brought him home to the house on Cross Street, safe and sound. When Frances and Clightie moaned about their homework, Kenny would madden them by saying, "Get on with it! You never know what might save your life one day!"

Clightie would thump her English homework down in front of him. "How could this save your life, Dad? How could it? Ever?"

"You never know," her dad would say again, and catch her eye with such sweet seriousness that she'd stop being mad at him.

"Where the blue wave rolls nightly on deep Galilee," mouthed Kenny, and now he felt so far away he could have been up in the sky, gazing down on himself standing in the clearing, his foot held fast, a silly rabbit caught in a murderous trap. "The blue wave rolls nightly—" and all at once the man's fingers loosened, fell away, his hand rushed up to shield his eyes. Kenny leapt; he bolted from the clearing, pounded up the track, seized his bike from behind the blackberry thicket, and rode away.

Not once did he look back. He'd kept his promise; he'd be home tonight.

At the very first factory he came to, Kenny was given work.

And when he later came to tell Frances and Clightie about that winter's day when he'd set out to find work, he never once mentioned the man beside the fire. He talked about the coldness of the morning, how his nose had gone numb and his hands frozen to the handlebars of his dad's old bike; he talked about how scared he'd been, how sure of failure, how he hadn't thought he had a chance in the world of getting any kind of job—and how he'd kept on riding anyway.

the city of love

1957

On a morning in the last weeks of the summer holidays, the phone rang in Frances and Clightie's house. They'd only had the phone connected last November, so it was still new and thrilling to hear it ringing from the hall. Wherever she was, Clightie would come running, heart pounding, hoping the call would be for her. Because it could be Charlie Grace, the clever, dark-eyed boy who sat across the aisle in math class. It could be that he'd thought of her in these long, dull weeks with nothing much to do, picked up the phonebook, and searched along the columns for her name. Once she'd glanced up from her algebra and found him gazing at her; the moment their eyes met he'd looked away. It could be him, Clightie thought whenever she heard the phone.

Her younger sister Frances came running too, getting under Clightie's feet, hovering when Clightie picked up the receiver, eyes wide, listening in. "It's not going to be for you," hissed Clightie, her hand over the mouthpiece. "Who's going to ring a ten-year-old?"

"Oh!" said Frances, and stayed there, her feet skipping on the carpet in a nervous little dance.

Frances was scared of the telephone; it sounded so shrill, so urgent, she couldn't help expecting bad news to come along the wire. She wasn't sure what kind exactly —something dreadful, certainly, a cold, sepulchral voice whispering words that would send their lives tumbling like skittles in a bowling alley.

Frances was afraid of everything. She didn't know why she was like that. Sometimes she thought a bad fairy had been present at her christening, bringing the invisible gift of a sinking heart.

"What are you standing there for?" demanded Clightie. "Go away!" If the call was Charlie Grace, Frances would be the biggest nuisance; she'd want to know who it was and what they said and then she'd probably blab to Mum. "Go away!"

Frances stayed. Clightie gave up. "Hello," she said into the telephone. "What? Pardon? What did you say? Ethel? There's no Ethel here." She listened for a moment longer, then shrugged her shoulders and handed the phone to

Frances.

Frances edged away. "Who is it?" she whispered.

"I don't know, do I?" answered Clightie crossly. "Here, you see for yourself. Go on!" She grinned unkindly, thrusting the phone at Frances. "It won't bite, you know. It's only some old lady; she's got the wrong number, I think."

Frances took the shiny black receiver and held it to her ear. The voice she heard was quavery and sounded very far away. "I'm coming to visit," the voice told Frances. "In a day or two. I'm coming to see Ethel."

"Ethel?" echoed Frances, just as Clightie had done. "We don't have an Ethel. Do you mean Irene? We have an Irene; she's my mum. Do you want to talk to Irene Sinclair?"

The little voice grew more distant, and crackles sounded between the words. "Friend," Frances caught. "Best friend," and then "Ethel" again, and finally, "Is Irene there?"

"I'll get her for you," said Frances, but Clightie was already doing it.

"Mum!" she yelled out down the hall. "Mum! There's some old lady on the phone who wants to talk to you!"

"That was your great-aunt May," their mother told them as she put down the phone. "She's coming for a visit at the end of the week." In a lower voice, almost as if she were talking to herself, Irene added, "It will give poor Cousin Pattie a break."

"A break from what?" asked Clightie, but before Irene had a chance to reply, Frances interrupted. "She said she was coming to see her best friend, Ethel."

"Oh, she won't be able to do that," answered Irene. "Ethel passed away years ago."

"Passed away? You mean—died? Doesn't Aunty May know?"

"Oh yes," replied her mother. "Only she's forgotten, I expect."

How could you forget that your best friend had died? wondered Frances, and she was just about to ask when Clightie demanded, "Where's she going to sleep?"

Clightie knew the answer to that, of course; she'd known it the minute the visit had been mentioned. Aunty May would sleep in Frances's small room, and Frances would move in with Clightie, on the old camp bed they kept beneath the house. It happened every time they had a visitor. "I hate sleeping in the same room with Frances," she grizzled to Irene. "I never get any sleep. She talks to herself. She whispers, on and on and on!"

"No I don't," said Frances quickly.

"Yes you do. Whisper whisper whisper," mimicked Clightie cruelly. "You sound like a—like a live mouse someone's wrapped up in tissue paper, scrabbling and scrabbling, trying to get out!"

"I do not!" cried Frances, her face turning hot and pink.

"Whispering?" echoed Irene wonderingly. "What do you whisper about, Frances?"

"Nothing! I mean, it's—stuff for school, things I have to learn by heart."

"No it isn't," crowed Clightie.

"It is!"

Irene sighed and left them to it, escaping to the kitchen. "Is," "Isn't"—they could keep it up for hours.

"Oh well," sighed Irene, and set about the breakfast dishes, clattering them extra loudly to drown out the shouting in the hall. "It is so things I have to learn for school!" Frances was shrieking.

"Course it's not. Little fibber! As if a primary school kid has to learn stuff in the Christmas holidays!" Clightie's eyes narrowed, fixing on her sister's face. "I know. It's—"

Frances froze, waiting. Did Clightie know what she whispered? She might. Clightie always found your worst, most shameful secrets.

"It's something to do with you being such a little scaredy-cat," said Clightie, and then Frances saw she didn't really know, otherwise she'd have said so, right out loud: that was what Clightie did with secrets.

"You're a baby," sneered Clightie. "Scared of everything."

"I am not."

"Am not, am not," mimicked Clightie. "That's what babies say."

Frances felt hot tears gathering in her eyes. "I hate you!" she burst out.

"And I hate you."

"I wish I'd never had a sister," cried Frances. "Not one like you, anyway!" Her head whirling, her stomach churning, she spun away from Clightie and ran down the hall, out the back door, across the yard, through the gap in the fence, and down the lane.

Clightie stood still for a moment, and then she ran too, up the hall and out the front door, along the path and through the gate, across the park into the streets on the other side. They ran and ran, till somehow the anger melted and they turned back home again, where for a little while they spoke to each other in strange, polite voices that didn't sound real, as if they were distant acquaintances, meeting in the street.

As she ran, thoughts whirled and tumbled round in Frances's head, like clothes spinning inside Mum's washer. Trust Clightie to remember about the whispering, even though it was a full six months since Frances had last shared her room. What Clightie didn't know, what no one knew and never would if Frances could help it, was that the whispering was prayers.

Frances couldn't get to sleep at night until she'd said a prayer for everyone—not only for her mum and dad and sister, but for all their relatives and friends and neighbors, and the kids at school and their mums and dads and sisters and brothers, so nothing bad would happen to them. She prayed to keep the world safe too—from wars and plagues and famines, from floods and hurricanes and fires, tidal waves... The long, long list kept Frances wide awake and whispering for hours. And always, just when she thought she'd finished, sunk her head down on the pillow and pulled the blankets up, she'd think of something else. Like—like a meteorite hurtling downward from the sky, a huge, knobbly piece of some far-off planet crashing down toward the earth. Then she'd have to start again, whispering to keep the meteorite away. At breakfast there were shadows under her eyes and the box of cornflakes felt so heavy it might have been filled with stones.

It was all part of being a coward, Frances knew. She hated being such a scaredy-cat. Look how she made Dad stop the car whenever they came to a bridge, so she could walk across on tiptoe because she was scared the bridge would fall if she was in the car. When she reached the other side everyone was cranky with her except Dad. "You'll grow out of it," he promised.

But how long would it take her? She was almost eleven; this year she'd be in sixth grade, the next year in high school, and on the way to high school the bus passed over a bridge…

She'd never told them about the prayers, not even Dad. It was too—embarrassing. It was stupid, thought Frances, hating herself. Stupid and small and weak.

She hated Clightie more, though—Clightie, who was never scared of anything. She hated every little thing about her sister: the shape of her telltale mouth, the mean green shade of her sneaky eyes, the brisk brave swing of her sandy hair.

Three blocks away, loping down Merrylands Road, long-legged Clightie was hating Frances, too.

Aunty May was ancient and sprightly, and very, very small. So small she must buy her clothes in the children's department, thought Clightie scornfully—her frilly pastel frocks would look great on a six-year-old. She wore sandshoes on her tiny feet, and bright white tennis socks, their cuffs turned neatly down.

It didn't take long for them to figure out why Cousin Pattie had "needed a break." On the very first night of

Aunty May's visit, they'd found her in the kitchen at three o'clock in the morning, gray smoke billowing, frying sausages in a pan. "I'm getting the tea on," she told them happily as they clustered round the door. "Pattie's getting hungry, and Stan will be home from work any tick of the clock. See how dark it is outside? Must be nearly six; I can't think what I could have been about, letting the time run away with me like that!"

Stan had been Aunty May's husband, a very long time ago. He'd died years before Frances and Clightie were born.

"She's loony," Clightie said to her father a few days later. "Isn't she, Dad?"

"Confused," Kenny told her. "It happens to very old people sometimes; their memories go."

This sounded terrible to Frances. "Will I be like that when I'm old?" she cried.

"You're so selfish!" sneered Clightie. "Always thinking about yourself!"

Frances ignored her. "Will I, Dad?"

It pained Kenny to think of his younger daughter grown old, without him there to keep an eye on her. He gave Frances a quick, warm hug. "You'll be fine," he said, hoping she would be.

"What about me?" demanded Clightie, forgetting all about selfishness. "Will I be fine too?"

Kenny grinned at her. "You'll be the terror of the neighborhood!"

"Aunty was out in the street with her shopping bag last night," said Frances. "We heard the gate creak and we looked out the window and saw her—"

"We had to run out in our pajamas and bring her back inside," added Clightie. "She told us she was going to the butcher's to get some more sausages for Stan's tea."

"Oh dear," sighed Irene.

"At least she's forgotten about visiting her friend Ethel," said Frances.

"Thank goodness for that," replied Irene.

But Frances had spoken too soon. At lunch on Saturday, when her dad said, "Another cup of tea, Aunty? I think there's just one left in the pot," their great-aunt replied briskly, "Thank you, Kenny, but not for me," pushed her chair back, and got up from the table. "I have to get going now," she told them. "I'll pop into my glad rags, then I'll be off."

"Glad rags?" whispered Clightie. "What are glad rags?"

No one answered her. Irene put down her teacup. "Going somewhere, Aunty?" she asked uneasily.

"Only over to Ethel's place, dear."

Ethel's place! They froze.

"Ethel?" prompted Clightie, ignoring her mother's warning glance.

"Oh yes, it's Saturday, isn't it? I always pop over to Ethel's on a Saturday afternoon." And before any of them could say a word, Aunty May had slipped from the kitchen and was halfway up the hall. From the room that had been Frances's they heard the sound of wire hangers being pushed along the wardrobe rail.

"We'll have to tell her," said Kenny. "We can't let her go all the way over there and find—"

"No Ethel," finished Clightie heartlessly.

Taps were flowing in the bathroom now, and a snatch of song drifted down the hall.

"She might forget," said Clightie. "You know how she does. While she's in there, putting her glad rags on. She might come out all dressed up and not remember what she's dressed up for."

"Clightie!"

"Well, she might!"

But when Aunty May came swishing from the bathroom in her best mauve dress with the posy of artificial violets tucked into the belt, her wild white hair held neatly by a purple headband, she hadn't forgotten a thing. "Toodle-oo, I'm off," she warbled, waggling her fingers at them. "Don't wait up for me, I could be very late. Ethel and I always have a lot of catching up to do."

"Aunty," said Irene. "Aunty, just a moment."

"Yes?" Aunty May peeped back round the door. "What is it, Irene?"

The old lady's bright, happy face upset Irene. She couldn't think how to begin. "Er—"

Kenny got up from the table. "Aunty," he said gently, taking her tiny wrinkled hand. "Aunty, there's something we have to tell you."

Aunty May sobbed as if her heart would break. They'd never seen anyone cry so much. Big, splashy tears streamed down her cheeks and soaked into the table-cloth.

Even Clightie felt sorry for her. Poor thing, she thought—and she looked quite sweet all dressed up: the mauve dress was really pretty, with its little bunch of violets at the waist. It was a pity about the sandshoes, but perhaps when you were very old all you wanted was something comfortable on your feet.

"Why didn't anyone tell me Ethel had passed away?" demanded Aunty May. She'd quite forgotten that she had been told, all those years ago, and that she'd traveled across the city for the funeral. She opened her handbag and took her hanky out, blew her nose, and then shook her head briskly, like a person stepping from a swimming pool. "So Ethel never got to Paris," she said sadly.

"Paris?"

"Ethel wanted to see Paris before she died. The City of Love, she called it."

"The City of Love," echoed Clightie, and she saw a city bathed in misty light, smelled flowers in the air, pictured narrow cobbled lanes where you walked in the evening, holding someone's hand. "The City of Love," she repeated dreamily, and Frances glanced at her sharply, surprised there was no trace of a giggle in her sister's voice.

Aunty May dropped the folded hanky into her bag and clicked the clasp shut, firmly. Then she pushed her chair back and got to her feet again. "Well, I'll be off, then."

"Off?"

"Where to?" asked Irene faintly.

"Over to Ethel's place."

Shockwaves rippled round the table. "But Aunty," protested Irene. "Ethel's—"

"Dead," snapped Aunty May. "I know, you told me just now." She glared at her niece. "I may be getting on, Irene, but I haven't lost my marbles yet! I'm popping across to see Ethel's house again, for old times' sake."

"Oh, Aunty!" Irene sounded as if she were about to cry.

"I'm afraid the old house is gone too," Kenny told her. "They pulled it down a couple of years back. Built a big electrical store there."

"Electrical store?"

"You know," explained Irene. "One of those places that sells toasters and irons, and fridges and—"

"I know what an electrical store is, thank you, Irene." Aunty May sat down at the table again, her black eyes sharp and businesslike. "Did you say this store sold fridges?"

"Well, yes—"

"Now that's something I have to get before I go back home—a new fridge for Pattie; her old one's on the blink, leaking all over the floor. I thought I'd get her one as a surprise—one of those new Kelvinators, with the little freezer at the top." She beamed around the table; Ethel seemed quite forgotten.

Frances's prayers kept her awake even longer now. She had to wait till Clightie was asleep before she could begin, and she had new prayers, too: ones for Aunty May—that she wouldn't burn their house down or wander off into the night. "And please, God, don't let her remember Ethel again, and get dressed up to visit," whispered Frances, and then stopped, hearing the soft creak of a door and the brisk patter of her great-aunt's feet scampering down the hall. "Off to get the tea for Stan," decided Frances, but the footsteps went right past the kitchen and out onto the back verandah. Now the laundry door squeaked, passing over the bulge in the linoleum.

A long time passed. Could Aunty May have gone out? You could get out that way, through the laundry and across the backyard, over the fence and out into the lane. Was she going to Ethel's place? Or just—anywhere? Frances imagined her great-aunt strolling down the road, round the corner, across the Woodville Road— she'd walk and walk and walk, thought Frances, crossing roads and railway lines and—bridges, walk and walk until something really big got in her way, something she couldn't climb over or pass round. Like—a river, or if she traveled far enough, the sea. And then?

She got out of bed and tiptoed down the hall, across the back verandah to the laundry. She pushed the door open; the light was on in there and taps were flowing, the tub brimmed with sudsy water dripping to the floor. Aunty May was piling wet clothes into the laundry basket. Frances splashed across the linoleum and turned the taps off. "What are you doing, Aunty?"

"What does it look like?" retorted her great-aunt, hoisting the laden basket up onto her hip. "Open the door for me, will you? There's a good girl."

"But—"

"Get a move on, will you? I haven't got all day."

Frances drew the bolt back and followed Aunty May across the lawn toward the clothesline. She helped hang out the dripping clothes—Clightie was going to be hopping mad; Aunty May had washed her best pink satin blouse, the one with the label that said DRY CLEAN ONLY. When they'd finished, Aunty May wiped her damp hands on the front of her nightie, then looked up and smiled at the big round moon. "Lovely washing day!" she crowed delightedly.

Frances stared at her. Her aunty looked so happy! As if being all muddled up wasn't scary but the greatest fun —turning the night into day, stepping in and out of time like a little girl in a storybook, bringing dead people to life again and expecting them home for tea.

"What are you doing out of bed so late, Frances?" asked Aunty sternly, making one of her curious little leaps back into their ordinary life. "It's way past midnight, you know. What do you think you're doing out here in the garden in your pajamas?"

"Oh, I—I don't sleep very much," stumbled Frances.

"Don't sleep much? Nonsense! You're a growing girl!"

"I—" And suddenly, without in the least having meant to, Frances found herself telling Aunty May all about those prayers that kept her whispering so late. It was quite safe to tell her because Aunty May wouldn't tell anyone else; in half an hour, ten minutes perhaps, her great-aunt would have forgotten the entire conversation.

"Good heavens!" exclaimed Aunty May, when Frances had finished telling. "You'd better cut down on that, Frances! You don't want to get to the pearly gates and have Him say, 'Here's that child who kept me up all night, listening to her jabber.' One good prayer will be enough!"

"What one?" asked Frances.

Aunty May thought for a moment. Then she said, "Angels and ministers of grace, defend us!"

"Will that be enough? It sounds so short."

"Covers everything, though, doesn't it? And everyone."

It did, too, Frances realized, when she'd thought about it for a bit. It sounded right. "Oh thank you," she said gratefully, throwing her arms round her great-aunt, giving her a giant hug.

"No need to get carried away, child." Aunty May made a small shooing motion with her hand. "Off to bed with you now."

"And you too, Aunty. You're going to bed, aren't you? And not—anywhere else?"

Aunty May stared up at the moon again. "May as well

have a nap," she said. "Before Stan gets home for tea."

They went into the house together. "Angels and ministers of grace, defend us!" whispered Frances, climbing back into bed, and she fell asleep the instant her head touched the pillow, as she always would, from that night on.

Clightie was sunbathing. She lay on a towel spread over the prickly buffalo grass, wearing her new black Speedo swimsuit, her long limbs coated with Coppertone, a clownish white blob of zinc cream on her nose. Her eyes were closed; she was thinking about clever, dark-eyed Charlie Grace.

That time in algebra when she'd caught him looking at her—when he'd turned away, the back of his neck had flushed bright red. That meant something, surely? Though Charlie Grace had never actually spoken to her, Clightie was almost certain he felt the same way she did. Whenever she caught sight of him, unexpectedly, across the playground, she flushed too, and a dizzy, weightless feeling swept over her; she felt she could leave the ground and float upward, away into the sky.

Footsteps scrunched across the prickly grass. Clightie opened her eyes and saw her little sister standing beside her. She was wearing her swimsuit: a droopy, babyish thing that should have been thrown out years ago. A towel was draped across her arm. "How come you're here?" Clightie demanded crossly.

Frances blinked at her. "To sunbathe," she answered, and began to spread her towel flat on the grass.

"Why do you always have to copy me? Why do you always have to do everything I do?"

"I don't. I thought of sunbathing too when I woke up this morning. It was the first thing I—"

"Fibber!" snapped Clightie, and closed her eyes, shutting Frances from her sight. Now she wouldn't be able to think about Charlie Grace—she never could when anyone else was around. You needed privacy for that kind of thing and Frances had no idea of privacy; she followed you everywhere. Clightie stole a quick glance at her sister from beneath her lashes. Little pest. There she was, settling down on her towel, only inches away, when she knew very well she wasn't welcome.

Clightie scowled. As if the little pest had thought of sunbathing the minute she woke up! Frances didn't need to sunbathe. She had their mum's smooth olive skin which never freckled or turned red and peeled, which turned brown naturally, all by itself. She didn't need blobs of zinc cream on her nose. Frances had natural blond hair too, a pale gold honey color, instead of the sandy shade Clightie had got from Dad. It didn't seem fair. Blond hair and lovely skin were wasted on Frances;

there was no Charlie Grace in her life. She was only ten, too young to be interested in boys.

Frances lay down and closed her eyes quickly, before she began to cry. Clightie was so mean to her, always! Mean as anything! She *had* thought of sunbathing this morning, so there! Clightie never believed her, Clightie—

"Frances! Clightie!"

Their mother was standing on the verandah. She was wearing fresh lipstick, and she'd changed into another dress. "Are you going out?" asked Frances.

"Just over to Mrs. Privett's place for a few minutes," her mother answered breezily.

A few minutes! It was never that.

"Keep an eye on Aunty for me, will you?" said Irene.

"What?" Clightie and Frances sprang to their feet, mouths falling open in round, horrified shapes. "Mum! You can't go off and leave us alone with her! Anything might happen! We wouldn't know what to do!"

"I'll be back in no time," promised Irene.

They didn't believe her for a moment. Once Mum got to gabbing with Mrs. Privett…

"Your aunty's having her nap. She won't be awake for hours."

"But Mum—"

It was no use. Irene darted back inside the house.

They heard the tap of her high heels hurrying up the hall, the bang of the front door.

She'd gone. They looked at each other, and then, without a word, tiptoed to their great-aunt's room and peeped around the door. She was asleep, her white hair spread out on the pillow, the hump she made beneath the eiderdown small as a little child's.

"Imagine," murmured Clightie in a soft, unexpected voice. "She was once a kid like us, who went to school and stuff—"

It seemed barely possible. Astonishing.

"And ..." Clightie went on in that same surprising voice. "She was a girl who—fell in love, who got engaged. She had a wedding, think of it! With bridesmaids, and confetti—she was a bride, in a wedding gown, and orange blossoms, and—"

Frances stared at her sister; it was strange to hear hardhearted Clightie talking in this soft, dreamy way. Frances giggled nervously and said, "Do you think she wore her sandshoes at her wedding?"

It was the kind of remark Clightie herself might have made, but when Frances did, Clightie flushed and got annoyed. "You're such a baby," she sneered, and stalked out to the backyard. Frances followed.

They lay on their towels, side by side, not speaking to each other. The sun was warm on their eyelids, cicadas sang in the high branches of the gum tree. "Clightie is never, ever nice to me," mourned Frances as she drifted off to sleep.

She woke suddenly, to find Clightie tugging at her arm. "What is it?"

"Shut up and listen!" Clightie put a finger to her lips. From inside the house came the sound of footsteps and then the bang of the front door.

"Mum?"

"Course not," said Clightie. "It's too soon; you know she always stays for ages over there. It's Aunty May."

"She was asleep."

"Well, she's awake now."

The gate clanged. Clightie and Frances ran round to the front of the house. Down the street, almost at the corner now, a small figure dressed in mauve was walking rapidly away. "She's got her glad rags on," said Clightie. "I bet she's going to Ethel's place."

"Oh no!"

They hurried after her. "Aunty! Aunty!"

"Oh, there you are!" Aunty May turned, beaming at them. "You're coming too, are you?"

"Coming where?" They held their breath as they waited for the answer; perhaps their great-aunt was only going shopping, to the butcher's perhaps, to buy more sausages for Stan's ghostly tea.

"To Ethel's place, of course," said Aunty May.

Frances swallowed. Clightie said carefully, "Um, Ethel might be out."

Aunty May laughed. "Not on a Wednesday, dear. Ethel and I always visit on Wednesdays. It is Wednesday, isn't it?"

They nodded glumly. It was funny how she always got the day right, even when she'd slipped back half a century.

"Hurry up now or we'll be late; Ethel doesn't like to be kept hanging about!" She strode ahead briskly. They lagged behind, whispering to each other.

"What'll we do?" fretted Frances. "We can't tell her about Ethel being dead, not again!" This was the bad side of drifting in and out of time, she thought: how an awful thing like losing your very best friend could happen many times, and each time be new and painful again. "She'll start crying, in the middle of the street. She'll cry and cry and cry—"

"Oh, stop fussing!" snapped Clightie. "Ethel's house is miles away, it's up on Banksia Street; by the time we get there, she'll have forgotten."

"Do you think so?"

"Of course." But Clightie's voice sounded strangely uncertain.

For such an old lady, Aunty May walked quickly; in

no time at all they were halfway down William Street, passing Frances's school, where Clightie had once gone too. And their mum before her, and even Aunty May, long ago when she'd been little, before she'd grown up and married and moved away. "You used to go here, didn't you, Aunty?" asked Clightie conversationally.

"Where?"

"Here, to our old school."

Aunty May stopped walking. Her sharp black eyes scanned the building beside them, the tall, narrow windows facing right onto the street, the sandstone walls, the high-pitched roof with the figures carved beneath: 1881. A soft hum of voices drifted through the open window beside them: teachers were gathered inside that room, sorting books and planning timetables, writing "Tuesday, February 2nd" up on all the boards.

Aunty May heard those voices and her dark eyes flickered. She stepped to the window, grabbed the stone ledge beneath the sill, raised herself on tiptoe, and peered inside the room.

"Aunty," whispered Frances, "Aunty, what are you doing? Come away!"

Aunty May took no notice. Her tiny hands gripped the ledge more tightly. "Witches!" she hissed into the room.

The hum of voices ceased.

"Aunty!" They grabbed her arms and hustled her off down William Street. Frances looked back once, and there, at the window, she saw the angry face of her new sixth-grade teacher, big bad-tempered Mrs. Blacklock, blooming like a big purple dahlia above the sill. Mrs. Blacklock would mark her down, Frances knew. "Whatever you do," Clightie had warned her, "don't get on Blacklock's wrong side at the start, or you'll be on her wrong side all year long."

"Aunty, why did you do that?" gasped Frances when they paused for breath at the bottom of the hill.

"They were mean to Ethel," replied Aunty May. "Downright cruel. Just because she had a stammer."

"But they weren't the same ones!"

"Makes no difference," said Aunty May airily.

Clightie was grinning. It was all right for her, she didn't go to that school anymore, she didn't have to face Mrs. Blacklock on Tuesday, February 2nd.

And there was no chance their aunty would forget about visiting Ethel now, even if Banksia Street was fifty miles away. The glimpse of her old schoolroom had freshened her memory. All the way down William Street, up the Trongate, round the corner onto Hudson Street, she talked of her very best friend. Of the parties and picnics they'd been to when they were girls, dances, engagements, weddings. She remembered dresses they'd worn: the apple-green chiffon Aunty May's mum had made for her sixteenth birthday, Ethel's coral silk with the bodice embroidered with pearls. She spoke of long Saturday afternoons when they washed their hair and curled it and sat out on Ethel's verandah talking about boys. They sounded like Clightie and her best friend Melanie.

"We wore Evening in Paris," Aunty May went on. "That was our favorite perfume. It came in a little blue bottle, and that's how Ethel got the idea of going to Paris, see? She said the nights in Paris would be that color, that sort of violet blue—"

They were almost at Banksia Street now. "What are we going to do?" whispered Frances, grabbing at her sister's arm. Clightie would know, that's what Frances thought. Clightie would figure out something, Clightie always did. She was the elder, and she wasn't ever scared.

A few steps ahead of them, Aunty May's voice trilled on happily: "Ethel had such a crush on Harry Glazby! When she saw him she went all dizzy—I had to hold her arm really tightly, otherwise I think she'd have flown right up into the air—"

Clightie shivered. "Like me," she thought. Distantly, she heard her sister asking, "What are we going to do?"

Now they were turning the corner onto Ethel's old street. "It's the house next to the tennis courts," Aunty

May told them excitedly. "The big white house, with the stained glass picture in the door, and the palm tree out the front—" She squinted into the distance, shading her eyes from the sun. "Where's that palm tree gone?"

Frances shook Clightie's arm. "Tell her!" And then she saw that Clightie's chin was quivering, and her eyes had gone really big and shiny, as if she were about to cry.

"I can't," said Clightie faintly.

"What?"

"I just—can't. Oh, Frances—she's so old, and you know what? When she was talking about those dresses, and how they washed their hair, and—and the way Ethel went all dizzy when she saw Harry Glazby, she sounded like me. You'll have to tell her," finished Clightie.

"Me?"

"Please," whispered Clightie. Frances couldn't remember Clightie ever saying "please" to her before.

They'd reached the tennis courts. Next door, the big shiny windows of the electrical store glared brightly onto the street. Aunty May blinked at them, astonished. "What's happened?" she asked them. "Where's Ethel's house? What's this?"

"Now," urged Clightie.

"Angels and ministers of grace, defend us!" recited Frances silently, and then she stepped forward to face her aunty. She thought her voice would tremble, or stick down in her throat, but it came out strong and clear. "It's the electrical store, Aunty, the one Dad told you about. It's the shop they built when—when Ethel sold her house."

"Ethel sold her house?" Aunty May turned on them indignantly. "No one told me."

"It was only a little while ago, Aunty. She decided suddenly, and sold it, and—moved to Paris. She's living in Paris, Aunty, in a big apartment, right next to—"

"The Seine," finished Clightie, who studied something called French Culture at school.

"Paris!" Aunty May's face lit up with pleasure. "The City of Love! So she got there, did she? Ethel got to Paris, as she always wanted to? Oh, she'll be so happy there!"

They nodded fiercely. "She is."

"Just goes to show, doesn't it?" crowed Aunty May. "If you hold on long enough, you might get your wish after all. Funny old world, isn't it?"

"Um, yes."

"What's that I see?" Aunty May was pointing to the window of the electrical store. Something seemed to have caught her attention there. She moved closer, peering in through the glass. Ethel was forgotten again, for now. "Is that a Kelvinator?" Aunty May asked them. "See? That model in the corner? It's just the kind I had in mind for Pattie."

"It might be," said Frances, joining her aunty by the

window. "See, it's got that little freezer at the top. You could make ice cream in it, Aunty."

Behind them, a low keening sound burst suddenly from Clightie. They turned round. Clightie's hands were making strange small fretting movements down her sides. "We've come out in our swimsuits!" she cried. "We've walked all that way, through all those streets, looking like idiots! With everybody seeing us! Kids from my school—" Her voice caught, she stared down at her long bare feet, raised a hand to touch the sticky blob of her zinc-white clownish nose. She knew some busybody kid would tell Charlie Grace. For sure.

"You look lovely, dear," said Aunty May. "In that little swimsuit. And so does Frances." She smiled at them sweetly. "You're lovely girls."

"The City of Love," Aunty May told Kenny and Irene over tea. "That's where Ethel's living now! She's got herself this grand apartment, right next to the Seine."

Kenny and Irene nodded wordlessly, and their hands got very busy with their knives and forks. The happiness in their old aunty's voice had a strange effect on Frances and Clightie; it was almost as if Aunty May's words might be true, and Ethel really was living in the City of Love, standing at the high windows of her apartment, looking out at the shining waters of the Seine.

In their room that night, Clightie said to Frances, "That was good, what you did."

"What did I do?"

"Telling Aunty May that story about Ethel living in Paris." Clightie was blushing. Her fingers flicked gently at Frances's arm and then flew away; she'd never given her little sister a compliment before. "It was sort of— brave of you," she added in a thick, embarrassed voice.

Frances blushed too. "It wasn't anything."

Clightie grinned. "Now you'll have to go to Paris," she said in her normal teasing voice.

"What?"

"Well, Aunty May is going to wonder why Ethel doesn't write to her, isn't she? So you'll have to write. You know the sort of thing: 'Having a wonderful time in the City of Love, wish you were here! Love and kisses, Ethel.' And then you'll have to post it from Paris, won't you? So it will have the proper stamps and stuff." Clightie smirked. "That's going to be a really expensive trip; you'd better start saving up."

She was joking, of course, thought Frances. She had to be.

Very early next morning Frances was woken by a noisy clatter in the street outside. She kneeled up in bed and peered out through the window. She saw an enormous box, taller than a man, perched on the edge of their front porch. Outside the gate, a big truck was pulling away.

"The Kelvinator's come," she called across to Clightie. "They've delivered Cousin Pattie's new fridge to our place instead of hers."

"What?" grumbled Clightie, stirring unwillingly from sleep. She didn't want to wake up, not just yet; she'd been having this marvelous dream about Charlie Grace. "Charlie," she whispered. "Charlie."

Frances heard. She knew what that must mean. She leapt from her bed. "Who's Charlie?" she asked excitedly. "Clightie? Have you got a boyfriend, Clightie?"

Clightie jerked fully awake. Her sister's eager face was hovering inches from her own. "Get off!"

"Is Charlie your boyfriend?"

"I don't know what you're talking about," replied Clightie coldly. "I don't know anyone called Charlie!"

"But you were saying his name! I heard you! It sounded like, I thought—"

"Well you thought wrong!" Clightie brought the words out sharply, rat-a-tat-tat, like bullets, like gunfire. Frances drew back; it was hard to believe this was the same Clightie who'd been so nice to her last night.

"And don't you go blabbing to Mum!" growled Clightie. "Don't you dare. Don't you go telling her I've got a boyfriend, that there's"—the threat in Clightie's

voice turned to something very much like pleading—
"there's someone called Charlie Grace."

Charlie Grace. Frances took a deep, slow breath. It
was true then. Clightie did have a boyfriend. She
wouldn't blab on her, even though she was longing to
tell someone. Her best friend Jeannie, perhaps? Jeannie
would be thrilled!

But no. "I won't tell," she promised, meeting her
sister's disbelieving eyes.

"Yes, you will."

"No, I won't."

"You will."

Frances didn't argue any more. She knew she'd keep
Clightie's secret.

Keeping secrets was grown-up.

*read*ing pRoblems

1954 – 1959

On her first day in Big School, a tall girl with tangled bird's-nest hair came up to Frances in the playground. The tall girl wasn't in uniform like everybody else, the sky-blue tunic with the four buttons like shiny medals on the chest. Instead she wore a funny dress that looked like an old lady's, and a droopy pink cardigan, its cuffs gone stiff with grime.

The big girl stood right in front of Frances, her feet planted firmly apart, hands on hips, and stared.

"Do you know where babies come from?" she demanded.

Frances didn't know. She was only seven and there were no babies in her family; her sister Clightie had been four when Frances was born. She screwed her face up, concentrating, struggling to find an answer, because the big girl looked so fierce and stood so stolidly it was obvious she wouldn't go away until she had one.

Babies, thought Frances wildly. Mrs. Travers down their road had a new baby. In the winter Mrs. Travers had been fat; suddenly in the summer she'd got thin again, and then there was the baby in a new shiny carriage that Mrs. Travers wheeled proudly past their gate.

From eating? wondered Frances, remembering how very fat Mrs. Travers had been. Did babies come from eating? No, that couldn't be right, or men would have them too. From—suddenly Frances remembered the carriage. "That's an elegant carriage," her mum had said, and Mrs. Travers had replied that she'd got it from Grace Brothers. So—perhaps the baby came with the carriage, like those little plastic toys wrapped up in cellophane you found in the bottom of the cornflakes box.

"Grace Brothers," Frances told the big girl, who threw back her head and roared with laughter.

"This silly kid thinks babies come from Grace Brothers," she screamed out to the other little girls, who shuffled their feet and looked away.

Frances turned red. As soon as the big girl had shouted her answer out loud, Frances could hear how silly it sounded. Of course babies didn't come from Grace Brothers! She'd answered too quickly, with the first thought that came into her head, the way she always did when she was scared. Now she remembered the ambulance screaming into their street to take Mrs. Travers off to the hospital, and how her mum had said, "The baby must be on its way."

"F-from hospitals," Frances stammered. "Babies come from hospitals."

The big girl grinned and shook her head. "No," she said. "Wrong again!" Her large eyes, so dark a blue they were almost violet, fastened on Frances's frightened face. "I'll tell you," she offered, and moved so close Frances could feel the girl's hot, sticky breath against her skin. Her clothes smelled funny too—a strange musty smell like the cupboard under the sink at home, where her mum had once found a nest of baby mice.

The big girl reached out and grabbed the hem of Frances's new blue tunic between her fingers. She flicked it up high, right to Frances's waist, so everyone in the playground could see her underpants. The big girl pointed down between Frances's legs. "They come from there!" she said triumphantly. Then she let the tunic fall back down over Frances's wobbly knees, spun round on her toes, stopped still, and said, "The man gets out his willy—"

"Willy?"

A whistle shrieked across the playground, and a hush fell as a teacher strode across.

"Vonny Cooney!"

That was the big girl's name.

The teacher stood in front of Vonny Cooney exactly as Vonny had stood in front of Frances, feet planted firmly, hands on hips. She screamed at Vonny so high and fast that Frances couldn't make out the words; they sounded almost like swearing, though Frances knew they couldn't be.

Vonny was almost as tall as the teacher and she stared right through her with those big, dark violet eyes. She didn't seem a bit afraid, didn't hang her head or make excuses, didn't say a word, not even when the teacher suddenly slapped her hard across the face. The slap made an odd thudding sound, as if someone had thrown a big, heavy book down upon the ground.

On that day when Vonny Cooney told Frances where babies came from, Vonny was in fifth grade and Frances was in third. Several years later, when Frances and her best friend Jeannie Macpherson reached sixth grade, Vonny was there. She'd repeated fifth grade and now she was repeating sixth. She sat by herself in a desk at the front, beneath the teacher's table, right under Mrs. Blacklock's glaring eye. No one ever shared that desk. It was kept as a place of punishment for girls who talked or read comics underneath their desks, or made messy inkblots on the pages of their notebooks. Then the teacher would point with her ruler: "You may sit next to Vonny Cooney for the rest of the day!"

Vonny Cooney didn't know how to read.

Reading lessons took place first thing in the morning, and again in the last tired hour before the final bell rang. The reading went fast along the back rows where the girls sat who got good grades on Mrs. Blacklock's tests; it slowed toward the middle and crawled at a snail's pace by the time it reached the front. At Vonny Cooney's desk it stopped altogether, as if the snail had found a wide stretch of muddy water it couldn't get across.

Vonny could take ten minutes to read a sentence from the school magazine. A paragraph could crawl on for half an hour with Vonny stumbling over words, keeping the rest of the class slumped in their places long past the final bell. Even the simplest words gave her trouble. *The*, for instance, a word you learned in kindergarten— Vonny couldn't seem to understand the *th* sound. She sounded the letters separately: *t* and *h*. "Tee-hee," she read, in front of every *th* word. Tee-hee—like someone laughing in a comic book.

"Again," commanded Mrs. Blacklock while everyone sighed and shifted, their legs growing hot and sticky on the shiny wooden seats.

"Tee-hee."

"Again."

"Tee-hee."

Mrs. Blacklock's face would darken to a purple color, as if her head were slowly being boiled. "You're not trying, are you, Vonny Cooney? You're a lazy girl!"

Sometimes Mrs. Blacklock would get so mad her breath went whistly; then she'd rise from her table and charge at Vonny, her sharp-edged ruler quivering, ready to come down. Vonny made no sound when the ruler made stinging contact with her hand—or once, with the tender place where her neck rose from the edge of her collar. Her silence maddened Mrs. Blacklock more. Once she grabbed Vonny's hair and dragged her right across the room, kicked the door open, and pushed her out, like a bundle of something, into the corridor outside.

Vonny Cooney took it out on the girls in the back row, Frances and Jeannie among them, the girls who read their compositions out loud in front of the class, who wiped the board for Mrs. Blacklock and walked down the aisles handing fresh notebooks out. "It's not our fault," they told each other when Vonny Cooney struck. "It's not our fault she's dumb."

Vonny caught Frances on the way home from school and ripped two buttons off her tunic. She put them in her mouth and rolled them round like candies, then she spat them down into the gutter where they lay all wet and shining, glistening horribly with the stuff from Vonny Cooney's mouth. Frances left them there and ran off; there was no way she was ever going to touch Vonny Cooney's spit, and Vonny Cooney knew it.

When Frances and Jeannie stayed late to help Mrs. Wilkins in the library, Vonny was waiting for them in the empty playground. Hiding. They didn't see her. Jeannie stooped to get a drink of water and Vonny rushed out and smashed her mouth right down onto the bubbler. Then she ran away.

Jeannie's mouth was full of blood; it slid from her lips and trickled down her round white chin. Frances took her hanky and tried to clean the blood away, but more and more kept coming.

Jeannie was trembling. "Am I all right?" she asked Frances. "Am I all right? Am I?"

"Open your mouth," instructed Frances, "and let me see. Oh!"

"What is it? What is it?"

"She's chipped your front tooth," said Frances.

"No!" Jeannie's hand rushed to her mouth.

"It's only a tiny chip," said Frances. "The dentist will be able to fix it."

"No, he won't!" wailed Jeannie. She was a big girl, almost as big as Vonny. She wore her hair in long blond braids she flicked back when she talked, and her voice still held the soft burr of Scotland in it, where Jeannie had been born. Scottish people were brave, Jeannie said, but now her eyes were big and terrified. "He won't be able to fix it!" she wailed. "I'll have it always, all my life, like a—like a scar! Every time I look in the mirror, even when I'm really old, I'll see it! I'll see this scar Vonny Cooney made!"

The blood was still trickling from her mouth, mingling with her tears. She must have cut her tongue as well, though Frances didn't tell her so.

"I hate her," spluttered Jeannie. "I hate her I hate her I hate her!"

"So do I," said Frances. It was the easiest thing in the world to say. Everyone hated Vonny Cooney.

In second term a student teacher came to work with Mrs. Blacklock. Miss Browning, she was called, and her first name was Geraldine; Jeannie had spotted it written on the front of the new teacher's lesson folder. "Geraldine," the little girls whispered to each other, "Ger-al-dine"—they thought it was a beautiful name. They loved everything about Miss Browning: her soft voice and gentle smile, her full, swishy skirts and Lily-of-the-Valley perfume, the way she wore her hair, swept up from her shoulders, fastened with shiny combs.

One day in Silent Reading, something amazing happened: Miss Browning sat down in the empty seat beside Vonny Cooney. A hush fell over the class—why had Miss Browning sat there? Why? And what would Vonny Cooney do?

Vonny slid along the seat till she was as far from Miss Browning as she could get without tumbling down onto the floor. She wouldn't look at the teacher; she turned her face and fixed her eyes on the picture hanging on the wall. *Grace Darling to the Rescue,* it was called.

Miss Browning didn't seem to mind; she placed a bright new book on the desk and opened it, then she began to read. It took two whole days before Vonny turned her eyes from Grace Darling toward Miss Browning. A day longer before she slid from the edge of the seat, another before she glanced toward Miss Browning's book.

"She's trying to teach her to read," whispered Carrie Elton, eavesdropping as she walked past the desk with a handful of pencil shavings for the wastebasket.

"Some hope," hissed Jeannie. "She'll give up, you bet."

But Miss Browning didn't give up. Frances overheard them too, standing out at the teacher's table while Mrs. Blacklock went through her long division. "*Th,*" Miss Browning was saying. "It's really hard to get, isn't it, Vonny? I can remember how I always thought of the letters separately—*T,* I'd say to myself, and *h,* and if there was an *e* after them, I'd say 'tee-hee.' It took me ages to understand, and sometimes I felt like ripping up the book and throwing it on the floor, I'd get so mad! Do you ever feel like that, Vonny? As if you'd like to rip and rip—because of words, and letters, and how they won't come together? And the way you keep on thinking it might really be easy, if you could only figure out one tiny little thing…"

Vonny Cooney sat there silently, head down, picking at her fingernails. Now and again she snatched a quick, furtive glance at Miss Browning's book, and once she said something in her low, throaty voice, and the teacher smiled. On the way back to her seat, Frances thought she heard Miss Browning say to Vonny, "You can call me Geraldine." Had Frances really heard that? Or had she imagined it? Surely she'd imagined it, because why would Miss Browning, beautiful Miss Browning, tell stinky Vonny Cooney she could call her by her first name?

Teachers never let you use their first names, and even if, amazingly, Miss Browning did let someone, surely that someone wouldn't be Vonny Cooney.

Miss Browning left and Vonny Cooney went back to stumbling through her words. You could see she hadn't learned a thing!

On the way home from school Frances and Jeannie saw her sitting on the low brick wall in front of Mrs. Ryan's house, with Daffy Kevin. Daffy Kevin was old Mrs. Ryan's son, a big grown man with wrinkles round his eyes and patches of bristle on his cheeks and chin where Mrs. Ryan had missed when she was shaving him. She had to shave him; she had to do everything for him, Frances's mother said, because Kevin hadn't grown right. He grinned at you and slobbered; he couldn't talk properly. When he spoke, thick, globby sounds came out, as if his mouth were full of glue.

Vonny was writing on the bricks with a stick of colored chalk. "She stole that from school," said Jeannie, and Frances agreed, because where else would a person like Vonny Cooney get chalk? She never had anything you had to bring from home: colored pencils or a geometry set, money for Bird League badges or the class photograph. She'd snatched Carrie Elton's class photo and scrawled great inky crosses through every face except her own. "I bet she's writing rude words on that wall," said Jeannie.

She wasn't, though. It was very quiet in the street and even though they were on the opposite side of the road they could hear exactly what Vonny was saying to Daffy Kevin as they hurried past.

"And this is *h*, see? And when you put those letters

together, Kev, they make what you wouldn't expect. They make *th*. Can you say *th*, Kev?"

He couldn't, of course. The sound Daffy Kevin made was a kind of shout that could have meant anything. "Gah!" he blurted, and then "Goo!," like a baby might.

Vonny answered as if he'd spoken a proper grown-up sentence. "That's right. It's easy, isn't it?" She smiled at him and Daffy Kevin smiled back, because he'd smile at anything. "You can call me Vonny," she said gently, and that was when Frances and Jeannie started running, very fast and silently, because they knew if Vonny Cooney caught them listening in to that, she'd kill them both for sure.

"She was trying to teach Daffy Kevin to read!" gasped Frances when they were safely round the corner, out of sight. It was the sort of thing that should have set them giggling like mad, only—it was so unexpected, so surprising, that Vonny Cooney should try to teach anyone to read, let alone Daffy Kevin, that the giggles didn't come. They didn't even talk about it; the whole thing was so astonishing that for once they couldn't think of anything to say.

"Do you know where Vonny Cooney lives?" Frances asked her sister. Clightie had a passion for drawing maps; she'd made a big one of their suburb, marking in all the streets and houses and the names of the people who lived there.

"Vonny Cooney?" Clightie looked up from her book. "How come you know her?"

"She's in my class at school."

"What? You mean she's still there? In primary school? But she was there when I was; she's only a year younger than me!"

"She was held back," said Frances. "Twice. She's really dumb."

Clightie put down her book. "No, she's not," she said. "Vonny Cooney isn't dumb."

"Yes, she is. She can't even read."

"That doesn't mean a thing." Clightie's voice was scornful. "You can be really clever and take ages learning to read. Vonny isn't dumb; can't you tell?"

When Clightie said this, Frances saw she could tell. There was something about Vonny Cooney, something you couldn't quite catch hold of, or put into words—

"She lives on Queen Street," said Clightie. "Number thirty-four. Is she a friend of yours?"

"Of course she isn't!"

"Why do you want to know where she lives, then?"

Frances didn't have an answer. She didn't know why she suddenly wanted to see the house where Vonny Cooney lived. She couldn't work it out, it was—private.

"No reason," she told Clightie. "I just wondered, that was all."

She went there on Saturday. Queen Street was on the other side of the suburb; you went under the railway bridge, past the shops, and then across the oval to Sydney Road. Queen Street was behind the highway, and number thirty-four was right at the end. Frances stood behind a big tree on the opposite side of the road and stared across at Vonny's house.

It had rained the night before and this morning the sky was a marvelous shining blue; the grass on the verges and in the gardens was brilliantly green. Raindrops sparkled on the leaves of bushes and the petals of flowers, the paint on the fences and houses glistened like new.

There was no paint left on the house at number thirty-four. Its timber was weathered to a drab gray and a strip of rusty guttering drooped down tipsily beside the porch. There was no proper garden, only mud and weeds. The house looked out of place among its trim neighbors, a house that shouldn't be there, a mistake. Frances was reminded suddenly of the first day she'd met Vonny Cooney, the way her ratty old clothes had stood out among all those bright-blue uniforms.

The front door of number thirty-four was closed, lopsided on its hinges. If you pushed it open that smell would rush out at you, the smell that came from Vonny Cooney's clothes: the mouse smell, musty and dark and old.

In the gray yard a mob of little kids were playing, tumbling and rolling in the sticky mud. As Frances watched, a very small one in a shrunken singlet staggered to his feet and started bawling. His piercing cries shook the air, going on and on until the lopsided door swung open and a lady with a baby clinging to her hip stepped out onto the porch. It was Vonny's mum; you could tell because she was tall like Vonny and had the same tangled bird's-nest hair.

Mrs. Cooney stared wildly round the yard. It was as if she couldn't work out where the bawling was coming from, even though it was easy to see the little boy in the singlet standing in the mud with his mouth wide open and his fists rubbing at his eyes. "Stop that!" she yelled. "Stop it! Stop it! Stop it!" but the little kid went right on bawling as if he couldn't see her, either. "Vonny!" howled Mrs. Cooney. "Vonny! Come here!"

Vonny didn't come; the gray house sat lumpish in the mud, and you knew there wasn't anyone else inside. Mrs. Cooney sat down on the step with a thump, and Frances held her breath as the baby perched on her hip rocked and jerked and clung. "Vonny!" sobbed Mrs. Cooney. "Vonny, where are you? Come here!"

Frances burst out from behind the tree and fled away down Queen Street. As she ran she remembered something Jeannie's mum had said once: how Mrs. Cooney was "no better than she should be." What did that mean? The words didn't make any sense when you started thinking about them, because if someone was better than they should be, wasn't that wrong? Didn't that mean they were snobby and perfect and superior? So if Mrs. Cooney was no better, wouldn't that mean she was all right? Wouldn't she be like everybody else? Yet Jeannie's mum's voice had quivered with disgust.

No better than she should be, no better than she should be, Frances's feet spelled out on the pavement, running across the sports ground and on past the shops, till the words lost meaning and were like the marks and squiggles of long-division problems written up on Mrs. Blacklock's board. The more you puzzled over them, the less sense they made.

At the end of sixth grade Frances and Jeannie went on to Tarella, Clightie's school, three whole suburbs away. The snob school, everybody called it, because only clever children went there. Frances and Jeannie wore uniforms of bottle green, pleated tunics and white blouses, crested woolen blazers, hats and gloves and ties. They didn't know which school Vonny Cooney had gone to—

"Reform school, I bet," said Jeannie, though she was joking, sort of. The Domestic Science, that's where Vonny would be, and they shuddered, picturing Vonny in cooking class, setting fire to the stoves, scaring people every time she took a knife up from the bench. "Imagine her in sewing!" breathed Jeannie. "They have machines at the Domestic Science; she'd grab your hand and shove it under the needle—"

"She'd sew your fingers to a traycloth!"

"She'd pull your hair out and use it for embroidery thread!"

"We're lucky we didn't go there!"

"Lucky!"

After a bit they didn't think of Vonny anymore: there were no girls like her at Tarella, and she faded to a bad memory, harmless as a ghost; she couldn't get them now. It was two whole years before they saw her again, and when they did, they hardly recognized her. It was a drowsy December afternoon, close to the summer holidays. Exams were over, Christmas was coming, and they lingered on the way home from school, browsing through comics at the newsagent's, gazing at the dresses in the windows of Coco-Pedy's. They drifted into Woolworths and tried out the lipstick samples, then sauntered up the aisle to jewelry. There was no one behind the counter. Jeannie tried on a pair of sparkly rhinestone earrings.

"What do you think?" she asked. Frances shook her head. Jeannie tugged the earrings off and scowled down at her Tarella uniform. "Nothing looks good with this. You could be Miss Australia and—"

A low, throaty voice interrupted them. "Can't youse read?"

They swung round from the mirror. The sales assistant was back behind the counter, glaring. There was something familiar about that glare, and the face—and surely they'd heard that voice somewhere before? They stared at her for ages before they realized they were looking at Vonny Cooney. Or were they?

Because this Vonny seemed so different: this Vonny was a young lady in a neat black skirt and starched white frilly blouse, her soft hair swept upward, fastened with shiny combs. When she tossed her head a faint sweet scent of Lily-of-the-Valley drifted across the counter. Her big violet eyes—yes, it was Vonny, because who else in the world had eyes of that color?—passed scornfully over their Tarella uniforms.

"Can't youse read?" she said again.

"What?" said Frances. She felt dazed. Why was Vonny asking them that?

Jeannie didn't care why. Here was Vonny Cooney, who'd bashed them all through primary school, who'd pushed her head down on the bubblers and filled her mouth with blood. Vonny Cooney, who'd been held back two whole years and never learned to read, asking them if they could read!

"We can read," said Jeannie coldly. "We can read anything, you know that."

"Well then." Vonny pointed to a notice tacked above the counter. "Please don't touch the merchandise," she recited. Her glance flicked over their uniforms again. "And that means little snob-school kids as well. Little kiddies on their way home to their mummies, spoiled brats who've got nothing better to do than go into shops and fiddle round with things they're not supposed to touch. Playing dress-up, were you?"

Their faces burned. "Now listen," began Jeannie, but Vonny said sharply, "Clear out, before I report the pair of you."

"You can't report us; we weren't doing anything!"

"Yes you were. You were touching things, trying on those earrings, I saw. And it says up there"—Vonny waved her arm and a fresh wave of Lily-of-the-Valley drifted toward them—"please don't touch the merchandise."

Merchandise. It was a long, long word. Both Frances and Jeannie knew she wasn't really reading it. There was no way Vonny Cooney could ever read a word like *merchandise.* Someone had told her; she'd learned the sentence off by heart.

"Get!" Vonny drew back her lips in a snarl, revealing a row of perfect, even teeth. Jeannie's tongue sought the chip in her own front tooth, the one Vonny had made back in sixth grade which her dentist hadn't fixed. "So tiny no one will ever notice," he'd told her, but Jeannie noticed, it seemed huge to her. Through a red haze of anger something clicked inside her mind—how back in primary school she'd been able to do a perfect imitation of Mrs. Blacklock's voice.

She did it now. Pointing to the sign above the counter, Jeannie demanded in Mrs. Blacklock's threatening growl, "What's that word, Vonny Cooney?"

Something strange happened to Vonny then; her great eyes went still, she tossed her head like some hunted animal might, scenting danger in the wind. She stared at the sign as if she were back in sixth grade, crammed into her little desk with Mrs. Blacklock standing over her. "Wh-what word?" she stammered.

"That one!" Jeannie pointed again. "The one that starts with *m*. Read it for me, Vonny Cooney."

"*M*," began Vonny. "*M*, mer—" Her eyes fixed dully on the letters. This was the thing that had always puzzled Frances: how even when Vonny knew the word, when someone had told her, she still couldn't read it from the page.

"Come on, Vonny Cooney," scolded Jeannie. "You're

not even trying! You're a lazy girrrl—"

"Mer-mermaid," Vonny hazarded.

"Mermaid!" scoffed Jeannie in her ordinary voice. "What would a mermaid be doing on a sign in Woolworths, eh?"

When she heard this, Vonny snapped out of her sixth-grade trance. She stared around her, taking in the long heaped counters, the shoppers browsing in the aisles. She touched the frilly collar of her blouse, as if to check that it was real. It was.

She turned on them. "Filthy little snobs!" Her hand shot out across the counter, seizing Jeannie's arm, twisting the skin right round, digging her nails in deep.

"Ow!" gasped Jeannie.

"Let her go!" Frances wrenched at Vonny's strong fingers, trying to prize them away.

"Is anything wrong, Miss Cooney?"

They flew apart, their arms dropped by their sides. The supervisor was standing right behind them, eyes gleaming. "Miss Cooney? Can you explain?"

Vonny was silent. She raised her chin a little and stood waiting for Frances and Jeannie to tell.

She'd lose her job, they both knew that. She'd get the sack. And serve her right! She deserved to, didn't she?

"Young ladies?" The supervisor gave up on Vonny and turned to them. She smiled at their snob-school uniforms, their green pleated tunics, their hats and gloves and ties. Everyone knew the girls who went to Tarella had bright futures, stayed on to graduate, went on to teachers' college and the university. The supervisor was on their side. You could see how much she wanted to sack Vonny: it showed in the way her arms were folded smugly across her chest, the sly way her eyes avoided Vonny's face. She was waiting.

Yes, Vonny would lose her job for sure.

Covertly, they looked at her. Vonny stood very straight, her eyes fixed on some still point behind their heads. It was how she'd stood when Mrs. Blacklock had shouted, her ruler ready to come down. Only now there was something different: a flicker of fear in Vonny's eyes.

To see it made you feel sick, somehow. That losing her job could make Vonny Cooney afraid. Jeannie's hand went to her collar; her tie was choking her. Vonny Cooney didn't have a father—Jeannie didn't know why she suddenly thought of this, or realized, suddenly and sharply, that the dank, dark smell that used to come from Vonny's clothes was the smell of being poor.

Frances thought of the day she'd spied on Vonny's house on Queen Street, seen those little kids rolling around in the mud, the tiny one who'd stood up, bawling. And Mrs. Cooney thudding down onto the step, yelling for Vonny, calling and calling as if Vonny could somehow save her.

"Young ladies?"

Frances and Jeannie didn't have to look at each other; they knew what they would do. Jeannie hid her burning arm behind her back. "It was nothing," she said in a small voice. "Vonny was just—"

"Helping to fix Jeannie's watch," finished Frances quickly.

"It's got this weak clasp," added Jeannie. "It keeps coming undone. Vonny's our—" Her lips shook as she spoke the word. "Friend."

"From primary school."

Then they walked away.

Vonny wouldn't be grateful, they knew. She would hate them for seeing her afraid, she would hate them more than she'd ever done, hate them always.

Outside in the street they couldn't speak. They didn't ask each other, "How come we said Vonny Cooney was our friend?" or "Why did we do that?"

It was like the time they'd seen Vonny trying to teach Daffy Kevin to read, the sort of thing that stopped your tongue, which you puzzled over lying in bed at night, your thoughts taking twisty tiny tracks inside your head, crisscrossing, doubling back, going round in circles, reaching no safe and solid ground.

It was too—hard. It was something you didn't want to talk about, not now—not ever, perhaps. You didn't even want to be reminded. At the corner of Oriel Street, when Frances touched Jeannie's arm, Jeannie jumped.

"What?" she squeaked. "What is it?"

"It's all right," said Frances quickly. "I only wanted to ask you something."

"What? What?"

"Nothing important," said Frances. "Only—" She smiled shakily. "Do you want to get an icypole at the milkbar?"

Jeannie's face cleared. "Oh, yes! Let's!" She tossed her long, fair braids back briskly, as if ridding herself of something.

"Race you!" she cried.

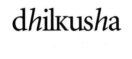

dhilkusha

1975

His history class had gone on late that afternoon, and though Kanti ran all the way from the bus stop it was almost twenty to four by the time he reached the gate of Raj's school. The street looked oddly naked without its familiar row of waiting cars, and the little knot of mothers who usually stood chatting by the fence had claimed their children and gone home to start the tea. Raj wasn't there.

The crossing lady was folding up her flag. "Did you notice a little kid waiting here?" Kanti asked her. "A first-grade kid—" He hesitated and then added, "A dark-haired boy, like me."

"Sorry, love, I didn't see." She waved at the stream of cars rushing down Wellington Road. "Had my eye on the traffic most of the time." She glanced down the side street where a last small gang of kids was straggling round the corner onto Laurel Avenue. "Perhaps he's gone home with a mate?"

Kanti knew Raj wouldn't have done that; their mother had told him he must always wait for his brother.

He turned in through the gate and hurried across the playground toward the Infants' block, knowing he'd find him there. It was the most likely thing in the world that Raj had been kept after school again.

A spindly palm grew by the steps, all out of place and on its own. Raj had told him a kid in his class called it "the monkey tree."

"And you know what he said to me then?" Raj had asked indignantly.

"What?"

"He said, 'And now we've got a real live monkey to go in it.' He meant me!"

Raj had thumped the kid. That had been his first fight at school. On his very first day.

Kanti had tried to explain. "Look, little kids—they always pick out the differences. If you were really small, shorter than the others, they'd call you Midget; if you had a limp, it would be Hoppy. They don't mean it, not really."

"Yes, they do," Raj had insisted. "They do mean it, Kanti."

"Okay. But they grow out of it, see? They get to know

more. The best thing is to ignore it, and after a bit they stop, they get used to you, they forget you look different."

"But I don't get used to them," Raj had said sternly, sticking out his lower lip. "Not when they're mean. And I don't want to."

Kanti walked past the palm tree, up the steps and in through the wide glass doors. Raj's classroom was halfway down the passage, opposite the art room, and his teacher, Mrs. Hopkins, was standing in the doorway, sipping a mug of steaming coffee. Behind her he could see Raj slumped at a table near the front of the room. He had his head down and was kicking at the table leg, *thump, thump, thump*—a maddening sound that had probably driven Mrs. Hopkins out of the room to stand there at the door. She'd have told him to stop and he'd have gone right on doing it.

Raj looked a mess. The collar of his shirt was torn; there was a bruise forming on his cheek and a cut above his eye, dark and crusty where the blood had dried. Mrs. Hopkins hadn't washed it or anything.

"What happened?" The question burst from Kanti abruptly, and it must have sounded rude because the teacher frowned at him. He added quickly, "Mrs. Hopkins?"

"Raj was telling stories," she said. "And one of the other children—confronted him."

Confronted. Kanti knew at once there'd been another fight. "Stories?" he echoed, puzzled.

"Lies. He was telling lies." The word sounded harsh, and Mrs. Hopkins must have realized this. "Fibs," she corrected. "He was telling fibs."

"Raj never tells—"

She cut him off. "Children do tell fibs," she said. "It doesn't mean they're bad."

"Raj isn't bad."

She ignored this too. "Telling fibs can be a way small children draw attention to themselves," she explained. "Particularly when they"—she glanced at Raj and then looked Kanti up and down, taking in his shabby state-school uniform—"don't have the advantages other children do."

She said this last bit—about lack of advantages—in the most ordinary way; she could have been talking about the weather, nothing personal at all. She didn't seem to have the faintest idea it might sound insulting. The awful thing was the way it made Kanti feel like defending himself, bursting into a long account of how his grandfather had gone to Oxford and his father was a doctor, even if he wasn't allowed to practice here. And how his mother spoke three languages and had been headmistress of a school that was a thousand times better than this crummy place where Mrs. Hopkins taught. And how the country they'd come from wasn't all thatched huts and jungle drums and monkey trees...

He didn't say any of it. He knew by now that Mrs. Hopkins might think such an angry speech hysterical; she could even think, like their neighbor Mrs. Twoomey, that the spicy food his people ate heated up their blood. He walked past her to Raj's table. "Hey!" he said, and his brother looked up at him. "Hey! What happened to you?"

"It wasn't a fib," Raj said, flashing a scornful glance at Mrs. Hopkins. "I wasn't telling fibs."

"I know." Behind him, Kanti sensed anger in the clash of Mrs. Hopkins's coffee mug down on the teacher's table. "I know; but what did you say that the other kid thought was a story?"

"It was our house! There was a picture of our house in the library book!"

Our house. For a moment, Kanti was baffled. They lived behind the milkbar their father had bought when they came here. "Small mixed business" was how it had been described in the newspaper column. "Opportunity."

"It's only till we get settled," their father had reassured them. "Till we work things out, and find our feet."

"The milkbar?" said Kanti. He couldn't understand why a picture of a milkbar had caused a fight. Unless Raj had insisted he didn't live in a shabby place like that.

"No!" Raj was shouting now. "The other house! You know!"

Shock prickled at Kanti's scalp. Of course he knew the other house, but he'd never realized Raj did. He hadn't thought his brother remembered anything from home; he'd been so little when they had to leave.

"You know!" Raj sketched an elegant shape with his hands. "Our house! The one where we used to live. It had white flowers on the verandah."

Jasmine. Kanti took a deep breath. He could almost smell the sweet scent of those small white blossoms, drifting through the windows of his old bedroom.

"It had a name," said Raj. "Our house. It was called something. It was called Dhil, Dhil—what was it, Kanti?"

"Dhilkusha," the older boy said softly.

That was the name of the house their grandfather had built when he'd first come to Kampala. It had been the name of a house he'd loved back in India, a summer bungalow in the small hill station of Mussoorie.

"Yes!" Raj clapped his hands. "There was a picture of it, of Dhilkusha, in this big book in the library. I opened the page, and there it was! And I said to Gary Burns, 'That's our house!'—and then..." Raj's voice faltered, then burst back loud and angry, "Gary Burns said, 'In your dreams!'"

Of course Gary Burns would say that if he saw a picture of Dhilkusha, thought Kanti. You could tell at a glance Dhilkusha was a rich person's house, so how could someone like Raj live there?

Raj jumped to his feet. "It was our house, wasn't it? We did have a house like that?" He sketched that graceful shape again. "With those verandahs? And the white flowers? And those wooden things on the windows, those—slatty things?"

"Yes."

"I knew!" Raj turned his glowing face to Mrs. Hopkins. "See! I told you, didn't I?"

Kanti fought back a smile. Despite the trouble Raj got into, it was hard not to smile at him sometimes—the way he'd been at school for nearly two years and never learned how you were supposed to talk to teachers. "And you said I was telling stories!" Raj scoffed at Mrs. Hopkins.

"Shh," whispered Kanti, trying to calm him. "Mrs. Hopkins believes you now."

"No, she doesn't." Raj began kicking at the table leg again. Thud thud thud.

"It's time you learned some self-control, Rajini Shah," Mrs. Hopkins said coldly.

"I don't want to! And you can't make me!"

The way the teacher's face puckered then, screwed up with distaste, reminded Kanti of Mrs. Twoomey again, of that time Raj had fought her son Jason outside the milkbar. Jason was bigger, eight years old at least, but Raj had beaten him. "Of course I know Raj can't help himself," Mrs. Twoomey had said to old Mrs. Evans who'd come out to the street to see what the noise was about. "It's in his blood, isn't it? Their blood is hotter than ours."

Their mother had been upset by that remark. "All blood is the same," she'd said to Mrs. Twoomey, and somehow Kanti had known she was thinking of that day in Kampala when they'd passed the Patels' store, smashed up—glass scattered on the road, and those thick, dark stains soaking into the curb.

"May I see the picture?" he asked Raj's teacher now.

She looked at him blankly. "What picture?"

"The one in the library book. The one of the house he's been talking about."

"Oh." Mrs. Hopkins sounded reluctant. You couldn't blame her, thought Kanti. It was almost four o'clock; she'd want to get off home. She wasn't old or anything, she probably had kids of her own. He knew he was expecting too much, at least for a kid in state-school uniform, with a brown unfamiliar skin. If he'd been a private-school boy, even a brown one—here Kanti caught himself up sharply; he hated the way he'd begun to think like this. It was insidious: drops of anger and humiliation wearing away at your heart.

"Please," he said in his father's gentle, cultivated voice, and saw the surprise in the teacher's eyes that such a voice should come from a boy like him. "I'd very much appreciate it, Mrs. Hopkins."

"I suppose it will only take a minute," she sighed, and they walked down the corridor to the library room. The book was on a high shelf behind the teacher's table. Raj spotted it at once. "It's there!" he cried, pointing, jumping up and down. "That's it!"

Mrs. Hopkins took it from the shelf and held it out of reach. "Clean hands!" she said to Raj.

He held his palms out; she frowned when she saw them and handed the book to Kanti. When he placed it on the table Raj darted at once to his side. "It's here! it's here!" he gabbled, helping to turn the pages.

"Careful," said Kanti. It was a big, thick book called *Houses of the World.*

On page eleven Kanti stopped turning. "See!" cried Raj exultantly. "See!"

It wasn't their house, but one so very like it—the same wide windows, the slatted shutters, the long verandah with the jasmine twining round the rails—that for a moment Kanti was back there, as if he'd fallen right in through the page. He was standing on the verandah looking down the shallow steps across the lawn; he could feel the smooth warm boards beneath his bare feet, smell the scents of roses and jasmine and sweet wet earth. It was early morning, the sprinklers were turning before the heat of day—and there was Rekha, skipping at the edge of the falling water, her little hands held out to catch the drops on her palms. "Kanti!" she called in her baby voice. "Kanti, look! I've got diamonds! See!"

Dhilkusha. It meant "place of the heart's gladness," and that was what Kampala had been for all of them.

They'd had to leave. Indians weren't wanted in that country anymore. It wasn't their country, they were told, even if they'd been born there and it felt like theirs and they had no other place. They didn't belong, and nothing they had belonged to them either; they'd stolen it from the country's true people, that's what they were told.

Kanti's family was late in getting away. Most of their friends had gone, packed into planes at the airport; but they'd stayed on too late. There was fighting through the country, and Kanti's father was a doctor; he'd thought he was needed there. The soldiers came for him early one morning, thundering at the door. "Go," he'd whispered to their mother. "Now. You must go."

They'd left that night, by train toward the border. Their mother had been nervous of the airport; she'd thought they might stop her there, detain her too, and take the children away. Kanti had only been eleven then, Raj was four, and Rekha hadn't turned three. They wouldn't have known what to do.

Their mother had thought the train would be safer, and it had seemed so, at first. They'd taken the slow train, the ordinary one that stopped at every little station, carrying people home from the city to their villages out in the bush. No one had been unkind to them, no one jeered or shouted; it had seemed they'd be safe.

And then Kanti had noticed something. People weren't smiling at Raj and Rekha the way they always did, even since the troubles had begun—those special smiles grownups give to tiny little kids. The brief gazes that turned in their direction had been grave and full of warning, before people looked away. They could have been saying silently, "Be careful, now…"

The soldiers boarded a few miles from the bridge. Kanti had taken Raj down to the end of the train while his mother settled Rekha to sleep. There was a bigger window down there—not that there was much to see, only the great starry sky and the dark country streaming past. Then the train had stopped. "Why?" Raj had wanted to know. "Why has it stopped?" Kanti shrugged; he didn't know himself. "To let some people off," he'd said.

They hadn't known about the soldiers until, above the clatter of the train, they heard their mother screaming. They ran, then. At the door of their own carriage, another traveler pulled them back and the big, solid bodies of strangers hid them from the soldiers' sight. Warm hands had covered Kanti's eyes; he had seen, all the same. He'd seen his mother standing, screaming. She had blood on her ears, trickling down over the lobes where her earrings had been. The soldiers were all around her, and one of them had Rekha in his arms. He was holding her up high, and then higher and higher, always out of reach. He was teasing their mother with Rekha, as Kanti and Raj used to tease their old dog Charlie with a bone. Only they'd always given Charlie the bone after a little bit. The soldier hadn't given Rekha back to them.

The train had begun to move again. Someone had smashed the window out beside their seat; its pieces were scattered everywhere. One moment Rekha had been there in the soldier's big hands, and then she wasn't anymore. He was holding nothing, then. Their mother sank down on the seat without a sound; the wind rushed through the window and the train roared on across the bridge. Even now Kanti could remember how all the noise had seemed to come from outside; inside the carriage there was a deep human hush, a sorrowful breath indrawn.

In the little library room of Raj's school Kanti closed the book called *Houses of the World*.

"See?" Raj tugged at his sleeve. "I was telling the truth, wasn't I?"

"Yes, you were." Kanti turned to Mrs. Hopkins. "We did have a house like that," he told her. Though she didn't say "in your dreams" as Gary Burns had done, he could see from her face she didn't quite believe him.

"When we lived in Kampala," he added.

"Kerala?"

"Kampala. It's a place in Africa."

"Africa." Now she looked puzzled, and he knew she was wondering why, as they were Indian, they'd lived in Africa.

"We had to leave," he told her. "So we lost our house, and—and everything."

"Oh?" She sounded uneasy now. "Yes, well—" She made a small, fluttery movement with one hand, as if to push their troubles away. They were nothing to do with her, those painful events that happened on the other side of the world. And they were no excuse for Raj's behavior either, no excuse for fighting and bad manners and lack of self-control.

They were like that, Kanti thought bitterly, these people they lived among now. They didn't want to hear. He'd watched them reading their newspapers in the trains and buses, skipping the foreign news, turning the pages to get to the other side. When bombs began falling and the news was on the front page, they didn't like it.

"Always trouble in those places," Mr. Twoomey would

grumble, collecting his *Sun* from the milkbar counter, scanning the headlines, disapproval on his face. "No self-control," his wife might have added. "But you can't really blame them, can you? Their blood is hotter than ours."

Kanti placed *Houses of the World* back on its shelf and then said to Mrs. Hopkins, "I think he should apologize."

"Oh, he has," she answered. "I saw to that. You said you were sorry, didn't you, Raj? For fibbing?"

Raj didn't answer. All the fight seemed to drain from him suddenly; he lowered his eyes and stared miserably at the floor.

"I meant the other boy," Kanti said to Mrs. Hopkins. "The one who said 'in your dreams.' He's the one who should apologize." And before she could say anything, he took Raj's hand and walked away.

The street where they lived now was flat and treeless; the moment you turned the corner you could see their milkbar down at the other end, the big plastic ice cream cone perched on its roof like an upturned witch's hat. When you walked through the door you saw the counter with the trays of candies under glass, the kinds little kids bought with their pocket money: mint leaves and musk sticks, cobbers and freckles and footie bubblegum. His mother kept getting them mixed up, and then the little kids would make her do it again. She spoke three languages, but the names of those candies just didn't seem to stick.

On the shelves above the counter were the groceries: Gravox and baked beans, flour and sugar and salt, sweet corn and pet food and breakfast cereals; posters for ice creams and Sargents pies glowered from the walls. They lived in the back, in four small rooms behind a curtain of plastic strips—it was as far away from Dhilkusha as you could ever get.

After Kampala they'd gone to London, where their father had joined them when he'd been released. Their mother had hated London: the cold, the way the dark came down in winter, the damp gray streets, the wet clothes freezing on the line. In some ways she liked it better here; there was something about the light on summer evenings which reminded her of home.

But she couldn't teach, as she'd done back in Kampala; her qualifications weren't accepted, and neither were their father's. He'd had to start studying all over again, and working at the Mail Centre on the night shift, because their milkbar didn't make much money.

It was the strangest thing to be poor, when once you'd been rich and strong. It wasn't simply the lack of all those things Kanti had once taken for granted; it was the way his present life never seemed quite real. In the mornings, when he opened the door on the street to take in the milk and bread, he half expected to find the garden of Dhilkusha, the dusty road beyond the gate, the different sky and air. He had this sense, all the time, that the world was flimsy and you could step right through.

"We did have a house like that, didn't we?" Raj asked suddenly. "Like the picture in the book?"

"Yes."

Raj squeezed his brother's hand. "Good. I thought so. I thought I remembered it."

"Did you remember it before? Before you saw it in the book?"

Raj frowned. "I don't know. I must have, though, mustn't I? Otherwise I wouldn't have rec, rec—"

"Recognized it."

"Yes!"

Kanti fell silent. What if Raj started remembering other things? He'd always thought Raj had been too little to have memories from Kampala, and they never talked about that time. In those rooms behind the milkbar, there was never a word spoken about their beautiful lost country, or Dhilkusha—so that sometimes Kanti did think it might have been a dream. They never spoke of Rekha, either, the little sister who used to wait at the gate for Kanti to come home from school. Rekha, who used to sing herself to sleep at night, sweet songs without any words, which drifted through the house and made everybody smile.

Sometimes Kanti almost hated his mother and father for never speaking of her, never saying her name, shutting her out; a poor little ghost left wandering, tapping at their doors and windows, crying, "Let me in! Oh please, please please, let me come in!" He understood why they were silent; it was because they were afraid. He was afraid for Raj now he'd seen that picture and remembered Dhilkusha. It might bring back things that were better forgotten—like the soldier chucking Rekha through the window as if she'd never lived or breathed or sung those wordless songs. Memory could be like those big anthills in the bush around their old home: leave them alone and a few stray ants might wander out, stir them up and savagery came swarming round your feet.

He knew he should leave Raj alone, but he couldn't stop himself. He had to know if his brother remembered more. "It was a beautiful house, wasn't it?" he prompted, and then stood waiting, tensely, to hear what Raj would say.

"Oh, yes!" His brother's face lit with a pleasure Kanti knew he wouldn't have felt if he'd also had memories of what had happened at the end. He didn't remember Rekha then, and though that was sad, perhaps it was good as well, because he couldn't be miserable about her. Raj grinned at him happily, picked up a long stick from the edge of the sidewalk and went skipping on ahead, rattling it along the fences.

Kanti walked on slowly. The thing he kept remembering was the soldier's face, the soldier who'd taken Rekha away. It was a young face, Kanti could see that now. A silly kid's face, flushed with a kind of pride—the sort of pride someone very poor and despised and young might feel if you gave him a uniform and shiny boots and a gun and then told him who to hate and blame for all that was bad and wrong. That soldier was no different from those kids Kanti could see now on the other side of the street, laughing and horsing around on their way home from school. Ordinary. Clueless. He'd got caught up, thought Kanti—if those kids over there had been in his place they might have acted just the same. It was an idea that always made him feel sick at heart: the way ordinary people might turn savage if you gave them the right occasion.

He quickened his footsteps. Up ahead, Raj was almost at the Twoomeys' house, and Kanti ran to catch him before he could rattle his stick along their fence. Raj didn't touch it, though; he'd seen Mrs. Twoomey out there on her front verandah, waiting for them to pass, hoping they'd do something she could pick on. She'd hated them long before Raj's fight with Jason; she'd turned against them that time Dad had asked her to stop Jason writing stuff on the back wall of their milkbar, stuff like "Asians Out!" and "Blacks Go Home!"

"Why don't you get back where you came from?" Jason

Twoomey jeered whenever he saw them in the street. Mrs. Twoomey had been really angry with their father; she'd said her son would never have written those words up on the wall. He knew right from wrong; he'd been brought up properly.

When they passed her house Raj raised his stick again because the fence next door had iron railings that made a lovely hollow sound. "I'm watching you!" Mrs. Twoomey called from her verandah, and Raj's shoulders slumped and his arm fell back to his side.

Her voice, and the way she waited to catch them out, made Kanti hate her. He knew he had to fight the feeling back; hate always messed you up. People like the Twoomeys were ignorant, that was all. Innocent, even. When they took the train, it was to go into work or into town for shopping or the cinema, not to flee for their very lives. The terrible thing that had come to his own family—the Twoomeys couldn't conceive of it; they lived in a country where such things didn't happen and they thought they never could. It was hard not to hate them sometimes, even to wish bombs would start falling so they'd know it could happen anywhere. And it was hard not to start thinking of them as "those people." He tried to keep himself from doing that; he knew it was part of a process: you started thinking "those people" and then they didn't count or matter and anything could be done to them. In Kampala, his own family had been "those people."

"There's Kenny!" Raj dropped his stick and raced on up the street. Kenny—Mr. Sinclair—and his wife Irene lived three doors down from the milkbar, and they were really nice. They'd asked Kanti's family to a barbecue: his mother had taken a tray of samosas and bhajis and a jar of mango pickle, too. Kenny and Irene had really loved that food! And the time Raj had the fight with Jason Twoomey, when their mother had said, "All blood is the same," Kenny had known what she'd meant by that. He hadn't thought she was weird.

"You've been in the wars again," he said to Raj now, catching sight of the bruise and the small cut on his forehead.

"You know what happened?" Raj asked eagerly.

"You tell me."

"This kid said 'in your dreams' to me!" Raj punched his fist in the air. "So I bashed him! Because he shouldn't have said that, should he? When you say something that's true, people shouldn't say 'in your dreams'! They shouldn't say you're telling lies!"

"No," said Kenny, his gray eyes serious. "They shouldn't."

A lady came up the path behind him. It wasn't Irene. Mrs. Sinclair was small and plump; this lady was tall like

Kenny, and she had the same round, freckled face and sandy hair. "This is Dolly," said Kenny, and the lady smiled at Raj and Kanti, her eyes crinkling at the corners in the same way Kenny's did.

"Just look at you!" she said to Raj. "What happened?"

Raj told her.

"I think you'd better come with me," said Dolly. "And I'll tidy you up a bit before you go home to Mum." She held out her hand to him.

Raj didn't take it. His eyes fastened on her red scarf. It was made of a fine, silky stuff and the breeze caught at it, sent it streaming, rippling—

Raj frowned. Kanti knew his brother hated the color red. He wouldn't wear anything red and he hated other people wearing the color, too. Their mother had a red sari blouse, and whenever she wore it Raj scowled, and if it was one of his cranky days he might start yelling for her to take it off. He yelled at Kanti's red T-shirt, and their father's crimson socks. They'd asked him over and over why he didn't like that color, but all he ever said was, "Because." He didn't know why, that's what Kanti thought; the frown Raj got when he saw something red was the kind you saw on kids' faces when a teacher asked them a question about a book they hadn't read.

"You don't like this, do you?" said Dolly now, putting a hand up to her scarf. Raj shook his head, and then Dolly whipped the scarf from her collar and hid it in her pocket, out of sight. "There," she said, smiling at him. "All gone." She held out her hand, and Raj took it this time.

While Dolly and Raj were in the bathroom, Kanti sat in the kitchen with Kenny, sipping a frosty glass of Coke. "Dolly's my little sister," explained Kenny. "She's visiting us from—"

Kanti never heard from where. Kenny went on talking while Kanti's brain stuck fast on those two words, "little sister." He'd heard them hundreds of times—the kids at school were always talking about their families. But somehow, this time—perhaps because he'd seen that picture in Raj's library book, and thought of Rekha— Kanti's hand trembled, drops of Coke spilled from his glass, and he began to cry.

It was years since he'd cried. The last time had been in London after their father had been released. It should have been a happy time, but when his father came out through the airport arrival doors alone, Kanti had started crying. He'd let himself believe that Rekha would be with him; he'd honestly believed she'd be there. For weeks and weeks, ever since they'd learned of the release, Kanti had told himself this story every night in bed: how Rekha hadn't died when she'd fallen from the train. How someone, some kind person living out there by the river, had found his sister and looked after her. And when his father got out of prison he'd find a letter waiting; he'd go off to this little village in the bush, and—It was amazing what you could make yourself believe when you were desperate. Anyway, his father had come through the doors alone at Heathrow, and that was the last time Kanti had cried.

Till now. Now he was crying again, in the Sinclairs' kitchen, when he was fourteen and far too old for tears. And too old for the words he found himself blurting out to Kenny: "I had a little sister once."

He didn't say more than that. He didn't tell Kenny how Rekha had died because it was too—terrible, too much the kind of thing people like Mrs. Twoomey thought they did to each other "over there." He knew Kenny wasn't like Mrs. Twoomey, he knew he'd understand—but somehow, Kanti had grown afraid to trust. "She died," was all he said.

Kenny didn't say anything for a long, long moment, and when he did, it was something Kanti would never have expected. "When my dad died," Kenny began slowly, "my brother Dan and I, we took his clothes off the line and hid them from our mum. We hid them in this box in the laundry; we didn't want her to see them." He added softly, "And you know what? I think we didn't want to see them either. We just wanted to put it all away, out of sight. You know?"

"I know," said Kanti. He saw how Kenny's face looked shy and uncertain, as if he thought telling this story mightn't be any help, but he was offering it all the same.

"We were only kids," Kenny sighed. "That's a silly expression, isn't it? 'Only kids'—as if when something bad or terrible happens to a child instead of an adult, it's never as painful, or real."

Their mother had had a bad day: Kanti could sense it the moment they came in through the door. She got really fed up sometimes, standing behind the counter all day putting those candies into little bags, making sandwiches and heating pies up in the microwave. And sometimes Mrs. Twoomey would come in to buy milk or bread and make one of those remarks their mother hated. "You're lucky, aren't you," she'd say, "to be allowed to come here? When there's so much unemployment?" Or she'd go on about Raj being cheeky to her.

Perhaps Mrs. Twoomey had been in today, because their mother got upset the moment she saw that Raj had been in another fight. "Fighting, always fighting!" she scolded. "Why are you like this?"

Raj always got sulky when she scolded. "No one's going to say 'in your dreams' to me!"

"In your dreams? What is this?"

He didn't answer her, not properly. He didn't explain

about the library book or the picture of the house that looked like Dhilkusha. He was afraid to, thought Kanti, and he didn't know why he was afraid. "No one's going to say it," Raj repeated, his voice rising on the words, his mouth taking on that crooked, snarly shape that always made Kanti think of tigers. "And if they do I'm going to bash them and bash them and bash them!"

His mother grabbed his arm. With her free hand she tipped Raj's chin up and gazed into his face. "Look at you! Listen to yourself! Listen to what you're saying! What do you sound like?"

He twisted away from her. "Like me."

"A little thug," she said bleakly. "That's what you sound like and that's what you're turning into." She sank down on the old sofa and began to cry.

They didn't know what to do. Kanti knew she cried sometimes at night; he'd heard her through the thin wall of their bedroom, and the soft murmur of his father's voice trying to comfort her. But she'd never cried in front of them before. "I can't bear it," she sobbed. "I can't."

Kanti patted her shoulder awkwardly. "Ma, don't. It's all right. Please don't."

She looked up at him. "No, it isn't. It isn't all right. He used to be the sweetest, gentlest child. Do you remember, Kanti? Do you remember how he was?"

"Yes. But listen, Ma, he's okay. He's okay now, he's not

turning into a thug or anything. It's just that—"

She wasn't listening to him. Her eyes looked funny, staring beyond him into some private place. And all at once, as if she'd forgotten how they never spoke of it, she began talking about the time when Raj was really small, before they'd had to leave Kampala. As if she were back there, walking through those other, larger rooms, the airy rooms of Dhilkusha, opening doors and raising blinds to let in the day, showing them all those things they'd had to leave behind.

Except for Rekha. She didn't mention Rekha once.

All this time Raj had been staring at his mother silently, an odd, absorbed expression on his face. Now he began shouting and his arm shot out stiffly, one stern finger pointing at her bright red sari blouse. "You're wearing it!" he screamed. "And you know I hate it, you know!" He rushed at her, grabbing at her sleeve. There was a long ripping sound as a seam gave way and a piece came free in his hand. He gazed at it for a long time before he dropped it on the floor. Then he rushed at her again.

"Raj!" Kanti grabbed at his brother's flailing arms. Raj kicked at him.

"Just look at him!" their mother cried. "He's like a wild thing!" She fingered the torn edge of her blouse. "Why does he hate a color? Why would anyone?" Her eyes were as wild as his. "Why?" she cried again.

"I don't know," said Kanti. "I've never been able to figure it out."

"Because," answered Raj, as he always did. "Because."

"Why do you keep saying that?" his mother demanded.

"Because, because, because—"

Raj went still in Kanti's arms. He tipped his head back against his brother's chest. Kanti felt the sudden, surprising weight of it. "Because," said Raj. "Because of— Rekha."

"Rekha." Their mother's hand flew to her mouth as if to push the name back in.

Raj wouldn't let her. "Yes! Rekha! She had a red dress! And red ribbons, here—" Raj touched lightly at the place above his ears.

Kanti had forgotten that. Forgotten the color of the dress his sister had worn that night, forgotten how her hair had been braided, looped, tied with red ribbons up above her ears. He'd forgotten how when the soldier thrust her small body through the shattered window one red ribbon had caught there, hung on the splintered wood for a second after she'd gone, until the wind had caught it and sent it streaming like a narrow banner away into the sky.

"Red," said Raj again. "Rekha was wearing red—in that train."

"Oh, Raj—" Their mother held her arms out and he

ran inside them. "Poor Raj," she whispered, and then looked across at her older son. "And poor Kanti."

"And Rekha," insisted Raj. "Rekha too."

They huddled together on the sofa, Raj on his mother's lap, Kanti close beside her. "She was my sister, wasn't she?" asked Raj. "And she was real, not just in my dreams?"

His mother nodded. "She was real."

"She's dead, isn't she?"

His mother nodded again.

"I thought so," said Raj slowly. "I thought she was, only I couldn't know ..." His fingers clutched tightly at his mother's arm. "I wanted to know. I needed to."

She stroked his cheek gently, and he said shyly, "I can remember her, I think. Just a little bit. She used to sing, didn't she?"

"Yes. She used to sing."

And as they sat there on the sofa, Kanti had a strange sense that their small, cramped living room had suddenly grown larger, the walls swept back, the ceiling risen high above their heads. There was space, and that same blithe airiness that had flowed through the halls and verandahs of Dhilkusha: as if in their shabby old milkbar an invisible door had been pushed open, and his little invisible sister had come dancing in.

*jerusal*ɛm *the* go*ld*en

1991

Frances went to Israel when she was thirty-six years old. Thirty-six! Back when she was fifteen, thirty-six seemed ancient to Frances: a wobbly old lady's age. She'd have died if she'd known she wouldn't even be married by then.

Frances had no intention of staying in Israel; her sister Clightie will tell you that. Red-faced with indignation Clightie still scowls: "She went on a working holiday! She said she'd be back in six months!"

Frances taught English on a kibbutz; there she met and married Nathan, and four years later their son Gabriel was born; now the small family lives in an apartment on Ramot Alon. Outside Frances's windows domes and minarets and spires float in a miraculous yellow light; Jerusalem the Golden, as she always calls it, has become her home.

Whose home, though? When Frances walks through the Old City she treads lightly; this place belonged to the Arabs once. Frances has always hated war. Now she's living in a country where there have been many wars and the threat of another is always with you, a slow cold creeping underneath your skin. She's joined the peace movement. In the evenings, while Nathan minds Gabriel, Frances trudges the streets and alleys of her neighborhood, climbs the narrow stairs of old apartment buildings, pressing bells and buzzers, knocking at doors, seeking signatures for peace. She carries a clipboard, printed pamphlets, and the precious pen her father gave her when she finished school.

Some doors slam in her face and angry voices tell her off, bellow out that she's a traitor and an Arab-lover—and a foreigner, too. What does she know? Who gave her the right to talk about peace?

Other doors swing open in welcome, spilling light into the gloomy passages and stairwells. An old man in a wheelchair tells Frances he'd be out there with her if he had his legs again.

"Sometimes I think I don't have the right," confides Frances, remembering those angry voices. "I wasn't born here. I'm not even Jewish—"

"You have the right," he says.

In a tiny flat above a shoe shop, even the baby signed. "He can't write yet," said his mother. "But I know he wants to."

An older child came running, a felt-tip in his hand. They inked the baby's finger and pressed it on the page.

But all this was Before. Now it's January 1991. To the north, Iraq has invaded Kuwait; as the months tick by and negotiations fail, everyone knows another war is coming. In a few days, it will be here. Sometimes Frances thinks she can hear it coming; there's a strange low buzzing beneath the sound of ordinary life, the hum of war fever, of madness gathering in the air.

It might be a chemical war, that's what the newspapers say. Will it be? Nobody knows for sure; they have to wait and see, and the waiting is terrible and full of fear. Gas masks have been issued, and in every house and apartment a sealed room must be prepared: windows bound with masking tape and plastic sheeting, and a rolled towel soaked in bleach placed in the gap beneath the door. When the Alert sounds, you have to go into that room, put on your gas mask, and wait for the All-Clear.

It's crazy, worse than any nightmare. Even as a scaredy little kid, Frances had never imagined a terror to match this: locked in a sealed room, waiting to see if you'll die.

Her husband Nathan, an expert on defense systems,

has been called away to Tel Aviv. Now Gabriel won't do a thing he's told; he's like that when his dad's away. He's being difficult about the gas mask; he won't even try it on.

"No!" He tosses it onto the floor.

Frances picks it up and slumps down onto the sofa. Her brain feels stiff and cumbersome, paralyzed with dread. She can't think of any story to persuade him, except the true one she can't bring herself to tell: that poisons might come seeping through the air.

Gabe runs to the window and stands staring out into the street below. "And don't you come creeping up on me!" he warns his mother. "With that thing!"

"I wasn't going to."

"Yes, you were. I know you."

Frances sinks back weakly against the cushions. "Gabe, I'm just sitting here, see? I'm not going to creep up on you."

He sneaks a glance at her. "You might be thinking of it. And you've got that thing in your hand."

"I haven't now." She flips the gas mask onto the coffee table. It doesn't look right to her; it seems flimsy, frail for what it has to do. She can't believe it will be any use at all. Like the plastic on the windows of the sealed room— how can you tell it doesn't have holes, holes so small they can't be seen? It's just ordinary plastic bought from the hardware store.

The dread she's been fighting back comes rushing over her again. What if she dies first? And Gabe's left on his own, lungs burning, struggling for each agonizing breath, choking, terrified, all by himself—Frances flicks her hair back and sits up straight; she knows she mustn't think this way.

Gabriel turns from the window. "Can we go to Jericho market? And get some figs?"

"It's not the season for figs, Gabe. It's wintertime. There wouldn't be any there."

"That man will have some—that man who's my friend."

He means the old Arab with the stall beneath the cedar tree.

"I don't think even he'd have figs in January."

"He will," says Gabe confidently. "So can we go? I'm sick of staying here."

"Not today."

"Why? Why can't we? It's Sunday, isn't it? We always go to Jericho market on Sunday."

"Not every Sunday."

"But lots of Sundays; we go"—he throws his arms out wide—"lots."

They do, too; it's a popular Sunday outing for families from Jerusalem.

"Not this Sunday, darling. Not without Daddy."

Mentioning his father is a big mistake. "When's Dad coming back?" he demands at once.

"Soon," says Frances vaguely.

"Is he coming today?"

"No."

"When, then? Is he coming on Monday? Is he coming on Tuesday? On Wednesday—"

She wishes she'd never taught him the days of the week. "He'll ring tonight," she says quickly, and this seems to satisfy him, because he turns back to the window, resting his forehead on the glass.

Frances gets up from the sofa. When he hears her move Gabe springs round, wary of the gas mask, ready to run.

She shows him her hands. "Look, they're empty, see?"

She stands beside him at the window, one hand resting lightly on the top of his soft, dark curly hair. When she looks through this window, out over Jerusalem the Golden, the thing that catches her eye, always, is the palace of the King of Jordan. It's unfinished, only partly built when the Israelis took that piece of territory many years ago. It has never been completed, and there it stands, every morning, patient on its little hill. Unfinished, like the lists of signatures she was gathering for peace. Unfinished, like Gabriel. The King of Jordan's palace is older than Gabe, it's stood there for over twenty years. Gabe isn't four, his birthday's not till March.

If March ever comes. That's the way she keeps on thinking now; the simplest little things keep on reminding her of the war. "Expiry date, April 21," it said on the tins of apricots she bought for the sealed room, and it made her go cold all over, wondering what might happen by April 21. "Angels and ministers of grace, defend us!" she'd whispered, placing the tins up on the shelf.

The street outside the windows is empty and very quiet. A single car goes by, that's all. Beside her, Gabriel begins his little chant, the one he learned from Joel and Ruthie Roth next door. "Saddam Hussein's a loony! Saddam Hussein's a loony!" "Stop it!" she longs to shout, because he doesn't really know what it means, this song about the Iraqi leader, how it's part of all the hate and war. He'll keep on singing it if she tells him to stop, so she says nothing and in a moment he stops of his own accord and says, abruptly, "I want it to be Before!"

"Before?" she echoes.

"You know!" He waves through the window at the strangely quiet street. "Like it was before, with all the cars and people and stuff, and—and Dad here, and going to Jericho market on Sunday, and buying my very favorite figs." He flashes Frances a sudden beaming smile. "My friend's got the very best figs in the world!"

"I know."

His smile fades; his hand shoots forward and grabs a fistful of her skirt. "It's all different now," he says, and then drops the skirt and clasps his hands over his ears. "The air is different."

The air. All along, Frances has thought she's the only one who hears that strange low buzz beneath the quiet, the hum of hatred gathering; now it seems Gabe might hear it too. He takes his hands from his ears and asks, "When is it going to be Before again?"

She can't think of an answer. "Um, when—" She falters, and he flicks her a quick, impatient glance.

"Will it be Before again on Monday? Will it be Before on Tuesday? On Wednesday, will it—"

The phone rings, mercifully.

It's Frances's parents calling from Sydney. Her dad struggles gamely to be cheerful, but her mum is almost crying. "Can't you come home?" she pleads. "The Embassy is sending people home, I saw it on the TV news."

"I can't," answers Frances. "I can't leave Nathan, Mum. And they mightn't let me bring Gabe, anyway." She doesn't say the rest of it: how, whatever it reads on her passport, she doesn't feel like an Australian anymore, Jerusalem the Golden is her home.

All the same, when she hears her mum's and dad's voices, pictures of her old home come crowding into her mind: she sees the floaty blue curtains at her bedroom window, the prickly grass of the backyard, the blistered paint on the front gate, the milkbar on the corner where the Indian family came to live. When she was little she thought she'd always live on Oriel Street.

Next her sister Clightie rings, and Clightie's voice has an angry sound. Like her little nephew Gabriel, Clightie always gets angry when she's upset. And Clightie is upset; she's been sitting home all day listening to the radio news, worrying about Frances and Gabriel, and when she went out to Safeway to get away from her thoughts, there was war news instead of Muzak playing through the store.

"Why did you have to break off your engagement to David?" she demands at once.

"David?"

"David Maxon. The boy you were engaged to when you were eighteen. Don't you even remember?"

Frances does. She gave David Maxon his ring back, still in its box. She even wrapped it, tied it with a bow. David Maxon thought it was a present. "For me?" he said. "Gee, thanks."

"David Maxon was goofy!"

There's a short silence before Clightie explodes on the

line. "If you'd married him you'd be living here. Why did you have to marry that idiot Nathan?" Clightie always calls Frances's husband "that idiot Nathan." She has never forgiven him for keeping Frances on the other side of the world, turning her only sister into photographs and letters and a voice on the telephone. Or Frances, for letting him. "Why did you have to marry him and stay over there?"

"Because—"

Clightie won't let her sister speak; she's too het up. "And why did you marry so late, and have Gabriel so late? So he's not even four—" Clightie knows she shouldn't say these next words, but she can't help herself. She's so afraid, and so ashamed of being afraid when she is safe here and Frances isn't, that she blurts them out. "And he mightn't get to be four! He might die!"

It's exactly what Frances has been trying not to think about all morning—and now Clightie has to go and say it, right out loud. "Why do you have to say that?" she asks angrily. "You've always done that to me, always: said exactly the worst thing you could think of, the thing I didn't want to hear. I hate you for doing that, I do. I hate you!"

"I'm sorry," gasps Clightie. "I didn't think. Look, I—" She doesn't get time to finish because her sister puts down the phone.

And then Frances does what she always did when she had a fight with Clightie. She runs. Clightie used to do it too. After they'd quarreled and shouted, they both ran from the house, Clightie through the front door, Frances out the back; they ran by different routes along the streets, to nowhere in particular, running to get away from the boiling angry feelings they stirred up in each other.

Frances grabs her purse and car keys, picks up the gas masks, takes Gabriel's hand, and rushes through the door.

"Where are we going?"

Frances says the first place she thinks of, the very place Gabe wanted to go. "Jericho market."

His eyes shine up at her. And why shouldn't they go? Frances asks herself. Why shouldn't they? What's the use of staying locked up in the apartment, waiting, afraid of what might come?

They meet their neighbor Hannah Roth coming out of the elevator, more rolls of plastic sheeting in her arms. "You're going somewhere, darling?" she asks, her eyes fastening on the car keys in Frances's hand. "Now?"

Gabriel beams at her. "We're going to Jericho market."

"Oh!" Hannah is dismayed. "Don't go there," she says to Frances. "Not now! The Arab market! What are you thinking of, darling? It's dangerous; it's an Arab place, they hate us. They always have, they want to sweep us into the sea. And now they think the time has come—"

Frances gazes at her friend's face, the flushed cheeks, the hot, hard eyes. Hannah gave her signature for peace; now fear has changed her mind.

"They're on his side." Hannah's voice sinks down into a hiss. "He's their hero, Saddam Hussein." The air seems to quiver round her words, and Gabriel hides his face in the folds of his mother's skirt.

Hannah sees and stoops down to him. "Oh, little one, I've frightened you. I'm sorry. But—you know what I've done, Gabriel? Last night? This morning?"

He lifts his face and shake his head.

"I've been baking cakes, Gabriel! Chocolate cake and halvah cake and sugar cookies, for Ruthie and Joel—and you. Isn't that nice?"

Gabriel nods silently and Hannah rises to her feet, adding in a whisper to Frances, "It was all I could do for them, give them their favorite things to eat. All I could do, when I started thinking we might all be going to—"

"Yes," says Frances quickly, before Hannah can finish, before she can say *die*. "Yes, I know."

Hannah turns back to Gabriel. "So, darling, why don't you come to my place, and your mummy, too, and share our cakes?"

"When we get back from Jericho market," answers

Gabe, and Frances takes his hand and together they step into the elevator.

Hannah gasps. They're going! To that dangerous place! The elevator doors close; Hannah presses the button, but she's too late; they've started down. She runs awkwardly to the window, the rolls of plastic bobbing in her arms, and peers down into the street. In a moment she sees Frances and Gabriel coming down the steps and running up the road toward their car. Running! Has Frances gone crazy? Hannah nods grimly. It's easy to go crazy at such a time.

Thousands of miles away, Clightie is running too. She rushes blindly along the quiet streets, past sprinklers turning in the gardens and high school kids drifting home from school, past a milkbar with frightening news placards outside.

She looks a total mess, hair straggling, tear stains on her cheeks, feet bare because she's run out from the house without her shoes.

Clightie doesn't care what she looks like; she's too upset about the way she spoke to Frances. If only she hadn't said that, if only she hadn't said that thing about Gabriel dying—it was bad, it was awful. Unforgivable. Clightie stops suddenly, sweeping back the damp strands of straggly hair. Unforgivable. But wasn't

Frances unforgivable too? Why did Frances have to say she hated her? Of course, Frances always said that when they were fighting, and Clightie said it too, but—Frances shouldn't have said it now. Now's different, now there's going to be another war over there. A big one. What if Frances dies in Jerusalem? What if Clightie never sees her again, never in this world? Never hears her little sister's voice again, even on the telephone?

A shiver runs through Clightie; it's the terror of the thought, and its strangeness, too. To wake up one morning and know, however wide the world was, Frances wasn't in it, anywhere.

What's that? What's that noise she hears? Clightie looks round; she finds she's right beside the park, and the noise she hears is laughter. Three high school girls are sprawled out on the grass, giggling and gossiping, yakking about some boy. "Oh, him! He's weird!" They look so happy, so carefree and untroubled, that Clightie is enraged.

How can they? How can they laugh, at this time? Don't they know what's happening in the world? Don't they know about the war that's coming, haven't they seen those pictures of the great gray fleets gathering in the Gulf? Of course they know, how couldn't they? They don't care, that's it, thinks Clightie furiously. They just don't care.

She feels like rushing at them, shouting—bawling them out, even grabbing one by the collar and shaking her up a bit. Yes! That tall blond girl with the high, shrieky laugh, the one who looks a bit like Frances when she was fifteen—that's the one Clightie would like to shake. She'll tell them off, anyway. She strides across the grass, ready to start shouting.

And then she stops. Suddenly she's thirteen again, walking home from school with her best friend Melanie. It's 1956; they live in an age called the Cold War. Clightie and Melanie don't know exactly what this means, they don't think about it because it makes them scared. Someone only has to press a button, their history teacher says, and the whole world will blow sky-high. And that might happen any time.

They pass by the newsagent's, and outside it there's a placard that says WAR. A single word, two feet high, which makes your stomach drop and the earth fall suddenly beneath your feet. They both see it, but they don't speak of it, walking on as if the placard hadn't been there, gossiping, giggling, talking about boys.

These girls in the park might be like that, decides Clightie now, and her anger dies away. They know about the war and they don't want to think about it, scared stiff, like she and Melanie had been. "Hello," she says gently, because the girls are sitting up now, staring at her.

"Hello," they answer shyly.

Nice girls, thinks Clightie, hurrying home to try to ring Frances again. Kind girls—they didn't giggle at her or smirk at each other, and she knows she looks a sight: her hair all over the place, no shoes, the baggy old shorts of Charlie's she wears around the house. Once she was slender like them, now she's sort of—spread. Her eldest daughter Jess is pregnant; Clightie will be a grandmother this year. Jess is sure the baby will be a boy; she's going to call him James.

James. A new person. But Clightie can't get used to the idea of being a grandmother. How can she be? In the mornings when she combs her hair in front of the mirror her middle-aged face is always a surprise. She expects to see the face she had in her schooldays, young and frowning as she struggled with the knot of her Tarella tie, while Frances banged on the door of the bathroom, shouting, "Hurry up, Clightie! Hurry up in there!"

It's less than thirty kilometers to Jericho and the road is as quiet as the street where Frances lives. Now and then a car passes on the other side, and a dusty old bus, heading for Jerusalem. Gabe's fallen asleep in the back, his head pillowed on the tartan picnic rug. Frances's eyes are blank; they always went blank after fights with

Clightie, when she ran down the lanes of their old suburb, feet pounding, heart bumping up against her ribs. And even though she's sitting in the car, quite still, her hands clenched on the driving wheel, Frances is running now. Running the way you do in nightmares, where if you run fast enough you can leave the terror behind and wake up in your own safe room. Frances wants to wake up in that place Gabriel calls Before.

"It's not Before!" He's awake the moment the car stops at Jericho market, his face pressed against the window, scanning the narrow streets, the dusty square. "I thought when we got here it would be Before."

"Let's go back, then." Frances is scared. Hannah Roth was right, to come here to the Arab market, at a time like this—what had she been thinking of? On ordinary Sundays the place is crowded, bustling; today it's almost empty. There aren't so many stalls in the square, and most of the shops in the narrow streets are closed and shuttered, even though the curfew doesn't begin for hours. The stallholders stand chatting together. The only shopper she can see is a tall Arab woman in Western clothes, choosing aubergines.

Frances pushes the key back into the ignition. "No!" protests Gabriel. "I want some figs! You said we could get some figs from my friend!"

"He won't have any, I told you."

"He has, look!" Gabriel points across the square to the stall beneath the cedar tree. His eyes are sharper than his mother's; all Frances can make out in that basket is a vague purple blur that could be anything. "I think that might be some other kind of fruit, Gabe. It might be grapes."

"It's not grapes, grapes aren't that big!"

She turns the key and he bursts into tears. It's not the angry, demanding crying of a child determined to get his way, but a soft, brokenhearted weeping, as if he's giving up hope of something dearer to him than figs. "I wanted them so much," he sobs. "So very, very much."

Frances turns the key back and the engine dies. "Why?" she asks him. "I know figs are your favorite, but—"

"That's not why!" he cries. "It's not because they're my favorite. It's not just that! I'm not a baby, Mum."

She almost smiles. "Then why?"

"Because they'll taste like Before." He leans over the back of the seat and grips her arm fiercely. "They will. I know!"

She thinks of Ruthie and Joel eating chocolate cake and halvah cake and sugar cookies, of their mother whispering, "All I could do, give them their favorite things to eat ..." "All right," Frances sighs, glancing quickly round the market. Is it really dangerous out there? As bad as she'd thought at first? It's empty and quiet, but no one looks threatening or hostile; the men round the coffee stall are smiling at some joke. She turns back to Gabriel. "But you stay in the car, okay? You stay here and I'll be back in a moment—with your figs."

For once he doesn't argue, only sniffs hugely and rubs at his eyes. "All right."

She locks the car and begins to walk across the square. Everyone is watching her. There's a group of men clustered round a radio; she hadn't noticed them before. She'd forgotten, too, how many times people have mistaken her for an American; it's not good to be an American here. A rush of panic rises to her throat; she has to stifle the urge to run. They won't harm Gabriel, she tells herself; whatever Hannah Roth may think, Frances doesn't believe they'll harm a child, even with that madness buzzing in the air.

The woman buying aubergines has turned to stare at her. There's no hatred in that stare, it's simply curious, and cool. Contemptuous maybe, but who could blame her for that? The fat man at the coffee stall—is he smiling at her, or at something his friend has said?

The square seems larger than it used to be; Frances is only halfway across when she hears, behind her, the unmistakable thud of their car door. She spins round;

Gabriel's pressed the lock and clambered from the car, he's running toward her—dancing really, waving his arms and twirling round on his toes. He's singing something. What? She can barely hear for the buzz of fear in her ears. It's—it's that awful little chant he learned from Joel and Ruthie. "Saddam Hussein's a loony!" he's singing, dancing across the cobbles, teeth flashing, eyes alight with glee. "Saddam Hussein's a loony!"

"Gabriel, stop!"

She reaches out, he dodges her hand and veers away, heading for the little stall beneath the cedar tree. "Saddam Hussein's a loony!"

There's a silence in the market that's whole as milk. The Arabs' faces waver and blur before her eyes; the only thing she seems to see clearly are the stones, so many stones scattered round, heavy, sharp-edged, ready to be picked up and thrown. Sinners were stoned to death in ancient times; Saddam Hussein's ballistic missiles are called Al Hijjara, which means stones.

"He's only little!" she wants to shout, but the Iraqi children who will die in this coming war are only little too. "Oh, don't hurt him, don't," she pleads silently. "Please don't."

A ripple of movement passes round the shops and stalls—stones, Frances thinks, stones—and then she hears a sound she barely recognizes because it's so unexpected. Laughter. A great wave of it, billowing round the square. The plump coffee vendor is doubled over, clutching at his sides. They think he's funny, this silly little boy. Funny, that's all.

She catches him beneath the cedar tree, beside the old man's stall. "Saddam Hussein's a—"

"Stop that!" she shouts.

"Loony!" He grins at her. "I've finished singing now."

There are figs in the basket, plump and luscious, gleaming on their nest of fresh green leaves. Where did they come from? In the middle of winter it seems a miracle they should be there.

"I knew you'd have figs," Gabriel is telling the stall-holder. "My mum said you wouldn't, but I knew." The old man smiles and leans across to ruffle Gabriel's hair. As the figs drop into the brown paper bag Frances is reminded of the skies over Baghdad, blue and empty now, from which the bombs will fall, sirens screaming, buildings falling into rubble, dust and smoke in the air. "I'm sorry, I'm sorry," she whispers helplessly.

The old man says nothing, but the gentle way he hands the bag of figs to her, and the faint warmth as their skins touch, fleetingly, reminds Frances of her dad.

On the way back to Jerusalem, at a high point overlooking the valley, Frances stops the car. She gathers up the sticky, sleeping Gabriel and walks to the edge of the road, gazing out over the stony desert and the low, round hills beyond. The soil is the exact same color as the felt board her first-grade teacher, old Miss Deely, used for religious instruction. As she told her stories from the Bible, Miss Deely would gently fix her small felt figures into the brown landscape: Mary and Joseph, Jesus and his disciples, Elijah and the ravens, the dove with the olive branch flying down to Noah's Ark.

And it's easy to imagine gods and saints and prophets once walked across this land. The blue sky curves softly over the desert, a huge hand cupping the earth inside. She can't hear that buzzing, that slow hum of madness gathering, anymore. The laughter in the marketplace, the old fruitseller's gentle hands, seem to have silenced it for a little while. She doesn't know what will happen in this coming war, but she doesn't feel quite so afraid.

Gabriel wakes, grizzling against her shoulder. "Where are we?" He stares out over the ancient land. "Are we in Before?"

"We're in Always," Frances tells him. "And now we're going back to Jerusalem the Golden to ring up Aunty Clightie."

chocolate *ic*ng

2002

His mum and dad had been laughing together at dinner-time, so James had felt tonight would be all right, but just as he was falling asleep the Noise started up down-stairs. The Noise—that was how he always thought of it, in great, thick black letters stamped inside his head. The moment he heard it, his stomach got this tight, full feeling, as if he'd had so much to eat he never wanted to eat again. His eyes snapped open and his hands shot out from the duvet and clamped against his ears.

There was a knack to blocking out the Noise. Hands flat over your ears didn't really work; the Noise still got through. You had to use your thumbs, press them in really hard, squashing the little ridges on the sides of your ears. Doors, James called them; he shut the doors.

The Noise blurred and almost disappeared, but it was uncomfortable lying in bed this way. After a bit his arms began to get stiff and his ears and elbows hurt. When he took his thumbs away, the Noise was still going on downstairs.

He wished he wasn't so scared of it. He wished he was brave like his great-grandfather Kenny had been. Grandma Clightie had told him all about Kenny: how when he was only a kid, not all that much older than James, his dad had died and Kenny had to go out and find work, in the middle of the Great Depression, to keep his family together.

The Noise seemed a small thing beside a bad trouble like that. He shouldn't be so scared. It seemed big to him, though—a different kind of badness, James thought suddenly, and somehow he knew Kenny had never known this particular kind of fright. Perhaps that might even be the reason he'd been able to be brave.

He took his hands from his ears and the Noise rushed in again. Earplugs, that's what he needed, like the ones he'd bought for Davie down at the chemist's shop. He wouldn't feel right about wearing them himself, though —with earplugs he might fall asleep and he couldn't risk sleeping. He needed to stay awake in case something happened.

He didn't know exactly what would happen, only that

this was the feeling the Noise gave him: a knocking like a warning in his heart, that something bad would come. Something far worse than Noise.

The very first time he'd heard it, James had been six, a year older than his brother, Davie, was now. When it woke him he'd got confused; he'd thought it was thunder, a storm coming in from the sea. Then he realized it couldn't be—there was no lightning flashing through the curtains, and the sea sounded sweet and calm. He'd sat up very straight and listened hard. When he'd figured out he was hearing his mum's and dad's voices yelling at each other, fighting, he'd been so scared he'd wanted to crawl under the bed.

It was a long time before he heard the Noise again; he'd been almost eight by then. Now the time between was getting shorter; he'd be eleven next birthday and the Noise was coming every second week. Davie had heard it for the first time ten days ago. He'd sat up straight in his bed, exactly as James had done. "What's that?" he'd whispered.

Davie was really little. You know those tiny kids you see starting Prep each year? How their schoolbags look too big for them? And how sometimes you see one standing alone in the playground, puzzled and looking around, like a kidnapped person waking in a strange room and trying to work out what kind of place he's in and what he's doing there? That was how little Davie was. And he'd had that same puzzled expression when he'd heard the Noise.

"What's that?" he'd asked again.

James hadn't wanted him to know. "It's the TV," he'd lied. "They've got it on really loud downstairs."

"No, it's not." Davie had switched on the bedside light and gazed sternly at his brother. "That's—it's Mum and Dad. What are they doing?"

James had been stuck for a moment. It's not as easy as you think to fool little kids.

"They're practicing," he'd said at last.

"Practicing?"

"For—for a play. You know what a play is."

"Sure." Davie had been in the school Nativity play last Christmas; a wise man in a long robe, his purple turban pinned together with Mum's best brooch. He'd even had a line to speak, and practice: "Lo, a star shines in the East!"

"Sure I know." The smooth baby skin on his forehead had creased into a frown. Then he'd shoved his duvet back. "I'm going down to see."

"No, don't!"

"Why not?"

"Because. You'd interrupt them. Interrupt their concentration."

"What's concentration?"

"What you need to do things properly."

"But—" Davie had slid from the bed, staring at the door, listening to the voices downstairs. The last thing James wanted was for him to go down there. He'd done that the first time. He'd crept to the bottom of the stairs and seen his mum and dad in the kitchen, looking different, like a pair of angry strangers who'd sneaked in from the street. People you didn't know at all. People you'd be frightened of.

"Tell you what, Davie," he'd said, struggling to keep his voice calm and ordinary. "If you get back into bed I'll read you a story."

Davie was crazy about stories; he loved them more than anything. At any other time he'd have jumped at the offer and climbed back into bed at once. But that night he'd hesitated, kept on standing there, his puzzled eyes fixed on the door, as if the thought of a story suddenly wasn't wonderful anymore. And this is what the Noise did to you, James knew: it stopped you from loving things.

He'd settled Davie back beneath the duvet and read him two stories in a voice that was louder than the Noise. And all the time Davie had kept on staring at the door. Halfway through the first story, the back door had banged like it always did at the end of their fights downstairs. Dad going out in the car.

Davie had given a little jump when he heard the bang. "What's that?"

"Just Dad locking up. They've finished practicing, and now they're going to bed, see?" James prayed Davie wouldn't hear the car start, tires crunching on the gravel, the squeal as it turned out into the road. He'd begun reading again, his voice loud as a shout, and after a bit Davie's head dropped back onto the pillow; he'd closed his eyes. But it was a long time before he'd gone to sleep—not until James had finished the second story and was halfway through the third.

He didn't want Davie to hear the Noise ever again. He didn't want him lying awake at night, he didn't want him to stop loving things. He didn't want his little brother to get like him.

"James has gone all quiet," Grandma Marie had said last Christmas. "He's not the child he used to be."

Grandma Marie made James feel uneasy. Her eyes went small and squinty when she looked at him, and though her voice was soft and she called him "lovie," he knew she didn't really like him. She didn't like his mum, either—"Jessica," she called her, instead of "Jess," and it sounded hard and cold.

"It isn't natural for a child to be so quiet," she'd gone on, spooning the pudding into bowls. "He's like a little old man. And such a long face on him—"

"He's growing up," Dad had replied irritably. "That's all. They don't stay babies forever, Mother."

James hated Grandma Marie. Grandma Clightie was his favorite. She took him and Davie out to all kinds of places, and she'd promised they could come with her next time she went to Israel to visit their great-aunt Frances and cousin Gabriel. But the thing James liked most about Grandma Clightie was the way she always saw the good in you, instead of hunting out the bad. "You'll grow," she'd said when he was worrying about being small for his age. "Your great-grandfather was over six feet, and he always said he'd been small as a boy."

"Was he quiet?" James had asked.

Grandma Clightie had thought for a moment. "A good kind of quiet," she'd replied.

James didn't want Davie to grow quiet. He liked the way his little brother was so noisy and cheerful, rushing laughing through the house; he liked how Davie jumped out of bed in the morning the minute he opened his eyes. He didn't want him to change. And that's why he'd gone to the chemist's shop the day after Davie first heard the Noise.

Their chemist was the kind of person who thought kids were a joke. The moment he spotted James he'd rushed over and leaned his elbows on the counter, grinning into his face. "What can I do for you, young fella? Heavy date with the girlfriend?" He'd winked at the people standing waiting for their prescriptions. "Bet this fella's after some sexy aftershave!"

"I want a pair of earplugs."

"Earplugs!" The chemist hooted. "She's a nagger, eh? The girlfriend? Or is Mum hassling you to do the washing up?"

A lady in a bowling uniform frowned beneath her hat. The chemist took no notice. "Or is Big Sister's so-called music keeping you awake?"

"Yes," James had said, to shut him up. "It's the music."

When you met people like their chemist you just couldn't wait to grow up.

Davie hadn't wanted to wear the earplugs at first. "They feel funny," he complained. "And you can't hear anything, except—rubber."

"That's the idea."

Then Davie's face went stubborn the way it always did when he was going to say "no" and mean it. The earplugs were the kind that came on a band, like headphones; he'd ripped them off and thrust them back at James. "I don't like this thing! What's it for?"

"It's a dream machine," James told him in a flash of inspiration. "See, Davie, when you wear it in bed at night you have these really great dreams!"

"Oh." Davie put them on again.

"Don't tell Mum and Dad, though. It's our special secret, okay?"

Davie grinned at him. "Okay."

They kept the Noise out, anyway. Because this very night, when James pulled his thumbs from his ears and heard the crash downstairs, Davie didn't stir from sleeping. The crash was china breaking, and James could tell from the sound it made—hard and sort of splintery—that it hadn't got a person; it had hit something solid—the fridge perhaps, or the kitchen wall. The back door banged; a moment later he heard the car start, then the skid of tires as it took that corner from the drive.

He didn't know where his dad went after they'd finished fighting. They lived in a small town; there was nothing open late at night and everyone was asleep. He'd just drive round, James figured, and the thought of his dad out there on those long, dark roads was a misery to him. It was another thing to keep awake for: the click of the door when Dad got safely home. Because what if he didn't?

Or what if something happened to Mum? Or—what if, what if, what if—the words made marching sounds, like his own footsteps hurrying home from school.

Almost running, his heart in his mouth until he burst in through the door and found Mum safely there. "What is it?" she'd ask sometimes, catching sight of his face. "Is something wrong, James?" He could never say, and that was the worst thing, almost: not to be able to say to anyone, not even to yourself.

Now the vacuum cleaner hummed downstairs; his mum was sweeping up the thing that broke. When it stopped he thought, "She'll go to bed now," straining his ears for the sound of her feet on the stairs. It didn't come; instead he heard the soft click of the back door closing. Dad? It was far too soon for him, and he hadn't heard the car. All at once the house had a cold, hollow feeling and James knew he and Davie were alone. It was his mum who'd gone out the door.

With a quick glance at the sleeping Davie he crept from his bed and hurried down the stairs. The hall and living room were dark; a narrow band of light shone through the gap beneath the kitchen door. When he pushed it open, his heart beating fast because this was the room where they'd been fighting, it was full of that swirly feeling that came on nights like this, as if huge invisible birds were flapping in the air.

The room was so clean and tidy it was hard to believe anything had happened there; all the plates and cups and pots from dinner had been washed and put away.

Nothing on the kitchen bench except for a big white mixing bowl, thick with chocolate icing, that his mum had left out for Davie to scrape clean.

He knew it was for Davie because Mum knew James didn't like chocolate icing now. Chocolate icing was one of the things he used to love and didn't love anymore. It was like he couldn't, somehow.

Where had Mum gone?

James ran to the window and pressed his face against the glass. The floodlights were shining outside; she must have turned them on when she left the house. He could see the whole garden: the lawn and trees and the wooden bench where she often sat to read. Sometimes when she was reading she'd glance up from the page and her face wore that same lost look as the new little kids at school, as if she didn't know where she was or what she was going to do.

Beyond the garden was the narrow strip of beach—and there she was: a thin, dark shape against the floodlit whiteness of the sand. It was good she was there; it was good to walk along the beach when you got upset. The sea sounded gentle, and if you walked long enough beside it you felt better: James didn't know what he'd do without the sea. In a little while, she'd come back in—

"What are you doing?"

He swung round and found his brother standing in

the kitchen doorway, rubbing at his eyes. For a moment he thought Davie was wearing a strange black necklace over his pajama top; then he saw it was the earplugs, the dream machine, slipped down from his ears.

"Just getting a drink of water." James snatched at the window blind to hide the garden from sight. It stuck halfway, as it always did, and then he realized it didn't matter because Davie was too short to see out the window anyway; his head only reached to the top of the sink.

"I want a drink of water too! I want—" Davie broke off, catching sight of something underneath the table, something his brother had missed when he looked around the room. Before James could stop him he'd grabbed it. "What's this?" he asked, holding out his hand.

It was a small piece of china from the thing that broke, with a thick brown smear along its edge that looked like blood. James snatched it and then saw the smear was nothing to worry about, only chocolate icing.

"What is it?"

"Just a bit of rubbish." James chucked it into the trash can. As the lid snapped open he saw more pieces of china in there, lots of them, and—and a cake. A whole cake, the one their mum had made that afternoon for the school bake sale. It was all smashed up.

"What's the matter?" Davie was right beside him, staring up at his face.

"Nothing." James shut the lid, quick.

"Where's my glass of water? I'm thirsty!"

"Sorry." James filled a glass from the tap and Davie drank it slowly, watching his brother over the rim.

"Where's Mum?" he asked suddenly.

"She's upstairs, asleep."

"Oh."

James couldn't tell if he believed him. Davie's head ducked down and then shot up again. "I had a dream," he said.

"Was it a good one?" James heard his voice sounding like Grandma Marie's, soft and full of lies.

"I can't remember." Davie put the glass down onto the bench and dragged the earplugs from his neck. He flung them down onto the floor. "This stupid dream machine doesn't work!"

"You just said you had a dream."

"I said I couldn't remember! It doesn't count if you can't remember!" He glared at his brother and then marched to the cupboard in search of the biscuit tin. While his back was turned James snatched a quick glance through the window. Mum had stopped walking now; she was standing at the edge of the water, staring out at the sea. That was all right...

"What are you looking at?" Davie spoke through a mouthful of biscuit crumbs.

"Just the garden."

He held his arms out. "Lift me up! I want to see the garden too."

The last thing James wanted was his little brother seeing their mum out there. He'd rush out after her; he'd notice she'd been crying. "Look," said James, trying to distract him. "Mum's left you all this chocolate icing in the bowl. I'll get you a spoon, eh?"

Davie shook his head. "I don't want it."

"What?" Next to stories, chocolate icing was Davie's favorite thing. "You mean you're too full, from dinner?"

"No. I don't like chocolate icing anymore."

A trickle of fear made the bowl tremble in James's hand. "You mean, just now you don't like it, or—"

Davie stamped his foot and roared, "I don't like it ever anymore!"

James's heart seemed to drop behind his ribs. It was starting, then: Davie was beginning to stop loving things. He stared down at the bowl in his hands. That icing! It was so rich and creamy and thick, the sort of thing any normal kid would love. It seemed like such a waste. "You might change your mind in the morning."

"No!"

James's eyes slid to the window again; he had to look.

He saw his mum walking out into the sea. He wanted to believe she was only paddling, dipping her feet in the shallow waves the way she did when they walked along the beach together. But there were no shallow waves tonight; it was cold and windy, the sea was rough and the tide full in. Already he could see only half of her.

He knew at once what was happening: the bad thing he'd dreaded coming ever since the Noise began. The bad thing that dogged his footsteps when he hurried home from school, that made him hold his breath tight as he rushed in through the kitchen door. He was always afraid he wouldn't find his mum there, that she'd have vanished, gone away from them. Like she was doing now.

He didn't know what to do. He wanted to rush out to her, get her back; but then Davie would follow, Davie would see. He had to get rid of him quick. "Davie, you go back to bed now, and I'll come up in a minute and read you a story." He gave his brother a small push toward the door.

"Don't!" Davie's small shoulders twitched his brother off. "Why are you talking like that?" he demanded, his eyes fixed on James's face. "Really fast, like gobble gobble gobble—"

"I'm not. Hurry!"

"Why? Why do I have to hurry? Why do I have to go to bed?"

James wanted to yell. He stopped himself; he knew if he once started, he'd yell and yell and yell, and he didn't want to be that kind of yelling person. "Please," he said softly. "Please, Davie," and the pleading in his voice startled Davie: with one quick scared glance at his brother he ran off up the stairs.

James jerked the kitchen door open and ran across the lawn. "Mum!" he was shouting. "Mum! Mum! Mum, don't! Mum, come back!" He knew she'd never hear him, not with the wind and the roaring sea. He couldn't bear to look out there, not yet—not till he'd reached the beach. He was too afraid she might be gone. He ran with his eyes fixed on the sky, and he saw a strange cloud up there beside the moon. It was shaped like a man hunched over a fire, and James had the strange feeling the cloudman was mocking him, whispering that nothing mattered in the world. The Noise and the fighting, Dad driving round on the roads, Davie getting scared, even Mum walking out into the sea—"Nothing matters," the cloudman whispered. "And you're a fool to care."

"Go away!" James hissed at him. "I hate you! Get away from me! You're wrong!"

The strange cloud broke up, drifted into smoke between the stars. And when James looked out across the floodlit beach his mum was there. She was striding from the water, she was right in near the shore! In a moment she'd be safe back on the sand. Coming back to them.

The most amazing lightness swooped right through him; he felt made of air. Joy—that's what it was. Joy. In his last English test, they'd had to give a definition of *joy*. "The feeling you get when the worst thing of all doesn't happen," James had written. His teacher Mrs. Atkins hadn't quite known what to make of that answer. She wasn't sure, she said, that it was a proper definition of *joy*. "Oh, it is," James had said, and she'd looked at him for a long moment and then reached into the drawer where she kept her box of gold stars. She'd pasted one on his test, right next to his definition.

His mum had reached the sand now; she was shaking the water from her hair and clothes. He longed to run to her, hug her tight, whisper thank you thank you thank you, for coming back to them. He didn't; he knew she wouldn't want him to know where she had been.

He flew back to the house. "You took a long time!" Davie yelled from his room when he heard his brother's feet on the stairs. "Are you coming now?"

"In a minute. I'll be there in a sec, Davie, and I'll read

you lots of stories." James paused on the landing to look through the small window there, check that his mum was still coming back. She was. She was in the garden now.

It was a beautiful garden; it was a beautiful house they lived in there. And his mum looked so lovely, walking beneath the floodlit trees, even with her hair and dressing gown all sopping wet. She was beautiful, everyone said so, and his dad was a handsome man. When you saw a photograph of them together, they looked like the kind of people who'd be happy ever after. He didn't understand why they weren't, only—it reminded him of the chocolate icing he and Davie couldn't eat anymore: a sort of waste.

And as he stood there the moon seemed to grow bigger and brighter, brighter than the floodlights lighting up the garden and the sea. It was so bright James could make out the line where the ocean met the sky— it was like a long, straight road. And along that road someone came riding, a boy on a big black bicycle.

James blinked. Perhaps he was dreaming, he didn't know. The boy seemed so real: a young boy, not much older than himself. And though he was so far away James could make out all these little details: how the boy's hair was the same sandy color as Davie's and his eyes were clear and gray like Mum's. He seemed familiar, even though he was wearing a funny old-fashioned jacket buttoned right up to the neck, a kind James had never seen before. The boy's breath came in small, smoky puffs, as if it were very cold on that long, straight road out there.

His name was Kenny, James was sure of that. And Kenny could see him too; he was looking right at the window where James stood, smiling at him, raising his hand in a small salute. "Ride on, James!" he called. "Just keep riding on!"

His voice was so kindly, so cheerful that James felt suddenly hopeful and brave. "I will," he promised; then he turned from the window, ran up the stairs and along the passage to the room where Davie was waiting for his story.